"What is it, *darling?*" Alexei taunted, the most fiendish smile curling the corners of his beautiful mouth. "Not enjoying this? It's no fun having to beg, is it? No fun having to crawl to someone you'd much rather die than even talk to."

Once more that searing gaze raked over her from the top of Ria's uncharacteristically controlled hair down to the neat, highly polished black shoes. It was a look that took her back ten years, forced her to remember how coldly he had regarded her before he had walked away and out of her life. For good, she had thought then.

"And I should know, angel—I've been there, remember? I've been exactly where you are now— begged, pleaded—and walked away with nothing. Tell me, what is the price of betrayal these days? Is it still thirty pieces of silver? Of course, you could try asking…"

Royal & Ruthless

The power of the throne, the passion of a king!

Whether he is a playboy prince or a
masterful king, he has always known his destiny:
duty—first, last and always.

With millions at his fingertips
and the world at his command,
no one dare challenge this ruthless royal's desire....

Until now.

Find out what happens
when duty clashes with desire

in

A Throne for the Taking
by Kate Walker
June 2013

And look out for

A Royal without Rules
by Caitlin Crews
August 2013

Kate Walker

A THRONE FOR THE TAKING

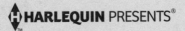

Recycling programs
for this product may
not exist in your area.

ISBN-13: 978-0-373-13157-0

A THRONE FOR THE TAKING

Copyright © 2013 by Kate Walker

Printed in U.S.A.

All about the author…
Kate Walker

KATE WALKER was born in Nottinghamshire, England, and grew up in a home where books were vitally important. Even before she could write she was making up stories. She can't remember a time when she wasn't scribbling away at something.

But everyone told her that she would never make a living as a writer, so instead she became a librarian. At the University College of Wales, Aberystwyth, she met her husband, who was also studying at the college. They married and eventually moved to Lincolnshire, where she worked as a children's librarian until her son was born.

After three years of being a full-time housewife and mother she was ready for a new challenge, so she turned to her old love of writing. The first two novels she sent off to Harlequin were rejected, but the third attempt was successful. She can still remember the moment that a letter of acceptance arrived instead of the rejection slip she had been dreading. But she really realized that she was a published author when copies of her first book, *The Chalk Line,* arrived just in time to be one of her best Christmas presents ever.

Because she writes romances Kate is often asked if she's a romantic person. Her answer is that if being romantic means caring about other people enough to make that extra-special effort for them, then yes, she is.

Kate loves to hear from her fans. You can contact her through her website, www.kate-walker.com, or email her at kate@kate-walker.com.

Other titles by Kate Walker available in ebook:

Harlequin Presents® Extra

THE DEVIL AND MISS JONES
THE RETURN OF THE STRANGER
  (The Powerful and the Pure)
THE PROUD WIFE

For the class of Fishguard February 2012.
Thanks for such a fun and inspiring weekend.

CHAPTER ONE

HE WAS COMING. The sound of footsteps in the corridor outside told her that. Brisk, heavy footsteps, the sound of expensive leather soles on the marble floor.

A big man, moving fast and impatiently towards the room where she had been told to wait for him. A room that was not as she had expected, but then nothing had been as she had expected since she had started out on this campaign, least of all this man she hadn't seen in so long. It had been more than ten years since she had spoken to him, but they would now be coming face to face in less than thirty seconds.

How was she going to handle this?

Ria adjusted her position in the smart leather chair, crossing one leg over the other then, rethinking, moving it back again so that her feet were neatly on the floor, placed precisely together in their elegant black courts, knees closed tight, her blue and green flowered dress stretched sleekly over them. Lifting her hand, she made to smooth back a non-existent wandering strand of dark auburn hair. Her style would be immaculate, she knew. She'd pulled her hair back tightly from her face so that there was nothing loose to get in a mess or distract her. Nothing to look frivolous or even carefree. That was not the image she'd aimed for.

She'd even fretted at the thought that her dress might
be a little too casual and relaxed when she'd put it on,
but the below knee length of the swirling skirt covered
her almost as much as the tailored trousers she'd considered wearing, and the lightweight black linen jacket she'd
pulled on over the top added a needed touch of formality
that made her feel better.

The room she sat in was sleek and sophisticated with
pale wood furniture. Far sleeker and much more luxurious
than she had ever anticipated. One of the soft grey walls
displayed a set of dramatic photographs, sharply framed.
In black and white only, they were the sort of images that
had made Alexei Sarova his reputation and his fortune.
They were superb, stunning but— Ria frowned as she
looked at them. They were bleak and somehow lonely.
Photographs of landscapes, places, no people in them at
all. He did sometimes photograph people—she knew that
from the magazines she had read and the stunning images that had appeared in the articles—but none of those
commissions were displayed here.

Outside the door, those determined, heavy footsteps
slowed, then halted and she heard the murmur of voices
through the thick wood, the deep, gravelly tones making
it plain that the speaker was a man.

The man. The one she had come here to meet, to give
him the message that might save her country from all-
out civil war, and she had vowed that she was not leaving
until she had done so. Even if the nerves in her stomach
tied themselves into tight, painful knots at the thought
and her restless fingers had started to beat an unsettled
tattoo on the wooden arm of the chair.

'No!' Ria reproved herself aloud. 'Stop it! Now!'

She brought her nervous hand together with the other
one, to clasp them both demurely in her lap, forcing her-

self to wait with every semblance of control and composure, even if the churning of her stomach told her that this was very far from the case. Too much rested on this meeting and she wasn't really sure that she could handle it.

Oh, this was ridiculous! Ria drew in a deep, ragged sigh as she put back her head and stared fixedly at the white-painted ceiling, fighting for control of her breathing. She should be well able to cope with this. She'd been trained practically from birth to meet strangers, talk with them, making polite social chit-chat at court events. It was what she could do as naturally as breathing while all the time keeping her head up high, her spine straight so that she looked as good as possible, with first her nanny's then her father's voice in her ear, telling her that the reputation of the Escalona family—an offshoot of the *royal* family—should be the first and foremost thing in her mind.

She could talk to presidents' wives about their trips round the glass-making factories, discuss the agricultural output of the vineyards, the farms. She could even, if she was allowed, converse intelligently on the vital role of exports, or the mining of eruminum, the new miracle mineral that had just been discovered in the Trilesian mountains. Not that she was often asked to do any such thing. Those important details were usually left to her grandfather or, until recently, to her second cousin Felix, the Crown Prince of Mecjoria.

But she had never before had to deal with any mission that meant so much in the way of freedom, both to her country and herself. That restless hand threatened to escape her careful control and start its nervous tattoo all over again at just the thought.

'Do it, then.'

The voice from the corridor sounded sharp and clear

this time, bringing her head up in a rush as she straightened once again in her chair. *Shoulders back, head up...* She could almost hear her father's strict commands as she drew in a long, deep breath to calm herself as she had done on so many other previous occasions.

But this wasn't one of those events. This man wasn't exactly a stranger and polite chit-chat was the last thing she expected to be exchanging with him.

The handle turned as someone grasped it from the other side. Ria tensed, shifted in her chair, half-looked over her shoulder then rethought and turned back again. She didn't want him to think that she was nervous. She had to appear calm, collected, in command of the situation.

Command. The word rang hollowly inside her head. Once she had only to command something and it would be hers. In just a few short months her life had been turned upside down, and in ways that made her status in society the least of her concerns, so that now nothing was as it had ever been before, and the future loomed ahead, dark and dangerous.

But perhaps if she could manage this meeting with some degree of success she could claw back something from the disaster that had overtaken her country—and family. She could hope to put right the wrongs of the past and, on a personal level, save her mother's happiness, her sanity, possibly. And for her father... No, she couldn't go there, not yet. Thoughts of her father would weaken her, drain away the strength she needed to see this through.

'I'll expect a report on my desk by the end of the day.'

The door was opening, swinging wide. The man she had come to see was here, and she had no more time to think.

As he entered the doorway her heart jerked sharply

under her ribcage, taking her breath with it. For the first time she felt suddenly lost, vulnerable without the ever-present security man at her back. All her life he had been there, just waiting and watching in case he was needed. And she had come to rely on him to deal with any awkward situation.

The *once* ever-present security man, she reminded herself. The protection that was no longer there, no longer part of her life or her status here or in her homeland of Mecjoria. She was no longer entitled to such protection. It was the first thing that had been stripped from her and the rest of her family in the upheaval that had followed Felix's unexpected death, and the shocking discovery of her father's scheming in the past. After that, things had changed so fast that she had never had time even to think about the possible repercussions of the changes and to consider them now, with the possible consequences for her own future, made her stomach twist painfully.

'No delays... Good afternoon.'

The abrupt change of subject caught Ria on the hop. She hadn't quite realised that his companion had been dismissed and that he was now in the room, long strides covering the ground so fast that he was halfway towards her before she realised it.

'Good afternoon.'

It was stronger, harsher, much more pointed, and she almost felt as if the words were hitting her in the small of her back. She should turn round, she knew. She needed to face him. But the enormity of the reason why she was here, and the thought of his reaction when she did, made it difficult to move.

'Miss...'

The warning in his tone now kicked her into action, fast. Her head jerked round, the suddenness and abruptness of the movement jolting her up and out of her seat so that she came to her feet even as she swung round to face him. And was glad that she had done so when she saw the size and the strength of his powerful form. She had seen pictures of him in the papers, knew that he was tall, dark and devastating, but in the 3D reality of living, breathing golden-toned flesh, deep ebony eyes and crisp black hair, he was so much more than she had ever imagined. His steel-grey suit hugged his impressive form lovingly, the broad, straight shoulders needing no extra padding to enhance them. A crisp white shirt, silver and black tie, turned him into the sleek, sophisticated businessman who was light-years away from the Alexei she remembered, the wiry boy with the unkempt mane of hair who had once been her friend buried under the expensive tailoring. Snatching in a deep, shocked breath, she could inhale the tang of some citrus soap or shampoo, the scent of clean male skin.

'Good afternoon,' she managed and was relieved to hear that her control over her voice was as strong as she could have wanted. Perhaps it made it sound a little too tight, too stiff, but that was surely better than letting the tremor she knew was just at the bottom of her thoughts actually affect her tongue. 'Alexei Sarova, I assume.'

He had been moving towards her but her response had a shocking effect on him.

'You!' he said, the single word thick and dark with hostility

He stopped dead, then swung round back towards the door, grabbing at the handle to stop it slotting into the frame. This was worse than she had expected. She had known that she would have to work hard to get him to give her any sort of a hearing, but she hadn't expected this total rejection.

'Oh—please,' Ria managed. 'Please don't walk out.'

That brought his head round, the black, glittering eyes looking straight into hers, not a flicker of emotion in their polished depths.

'Walk out?'

He shook his dark head and there was actually the faintest hint of a smile on those beautifully sensual lips. But a shiver ran down Ria's spine as she saw the way that that smile was not reflected in his eyes at all. They remained as cold and emotionless as black glass.

'I'm not walking out. You are.'

It was far worse than she had expected. She hadn't really believed that he would recognise her that fast and that easily. Ten years was a long time and they had been little more than children when they had last had any close contact. She knew she was no longer the chubby, awkward girl he had once known. She was inches taller, slimmer, and her hair had darkened so that it was now a rich auburn instead of the nondescript brown of her childhood. So she had expected to have to explain herself to him. But she had thought that he would wait to hear that explanation, had hoped, at least, that he would want to know just why she was here.

'No…' She shook her head. 'No, I'm not.'

Dark eyes flashed in sudden anger and she barely controlled her instinctive shrinking away with an effort. Royal duchesses didn't shrink. Not even ex-royal duchesses.

'No?'

How did he manage to put such cynicism, such hostility into one word?

'I should point out to you that I own this building. I am the one who says who can stay and who should go. And you are going.'

'Don't you want to know why I'm here?'

If she had thrown something into the face of a marble statue, it couldn't have had less effect. Perhaps his stunning features became a little more unyielding, those brilliant eyes even colder, but it was hard to say for sure.

'Not really. In fact, not at all. What I want is you out of here and not coming back.'

No, what he really wanted was for her never to have come here at all, Alexei told himself, coming to a halt in the middle of his office, restless as a caged tiger that had reached the metal bars that held him imprisoned. But the truth was that it wasn't anything physical that kept him captive. It was the memories of the past that now reached out to ensnare him, fastening shackles around his ankles to keep him from getting away.

He had never expected to see her or anyone from Mecjoria ever again. He thought he had moved on; he'd turned his life around, made a new existence for himself and his mother. It had taken years, sadly too many to give his mother the life she deserved as she'd aged, but he'd got there. And now he was wealthier than he'd ever been as a…as a prince, his mind finished for him, even though it was the last thing he wanted. He had no wish to remember anything about his connection to the Mecjorian royal family—or the country itself. He had severed all links with the place—had them severed for him—and he was determined that was the way it was going to stay. He would never have looked back at all if it hadn't been for the sudden and shockingly unexpected appearance of Ria here in this room.

He waited a moment and then pulled the door open again. 'Or do I have to call security?'

Ria's eyebrows rose sharply until they disappeared under her fringe as she turned a cool, green gaze on him.

Suddenly she had become the Grand Duchess she was right before his eyes and he loathed the way that made him feel.

'You'd resort to the heavy gang? That wouldn't look good in the gossip columns. "International playboy needs help to deal with one small female intruder".'

'Small? I would hardly call you small,' he drawled coolly. 'You must have grown—what?—six inches since I saw you last?'

She had grown in other ways too, he acknowledged, admitting to himself the instant and very basic male reaction that had taken him by storm in the first moments he had seen her. Before he had realised just who she was.

He hadn't seen such a stunning woman in years—in his life. Everything that was male in him had responded to the sight of her tall, slender figure, the burnished hair, porcelain skin, long, long legs...

And then he had realised that it was Ria. She had grown up, grown taller, slimmed down. Her face had developed planes and angles where there had once been just firm, round, apple-rosy cheeks. He had loved those cheeks, he admitted to himself. They had been soft and curved, so smooth, that he had loved to pinch them softly, pretending he was teasing but knowing that what he actually wanted was to feel the satin of her skin, stroke it with his fingertips. These days, Ria had cheekbones that looked as if they would slice open any stroking finger, and the rosy cheeks were carefully toned down with skilful make-up. The slant of those cheekbones emphasised the jade green of her eyes, and the soft pink curve of her mouth, but it was obvious that any softness in her appearance was turned into a lie by the way she behaved.

In a series of pulsing jolts, like the effect of an electric current pounding into him, he had known stunning attraction and the rush of desire that heated his entire body, the shock of recognition, of disbelief, of frank confusion as to just why she should be here at all. And then, just as the memory of how they had once been together had slid into his mind, she had destroyed it totally, shattering the memory as effectively as if she had taken a heavy metal hammer to it.

That had been when she had looked down her aristocratic nose at him, her expression obviously meant to make him feel less than the dirt beneath her neatly-shod feet. And Ria, who had once been his friend and confidant, Ria who he had just recognised as a sweet girl who had grown into a stunningly sensual woman, had become once more the Ria who together with her father and her family had stuck a knife in his back, ruined his mother's life and cast them out into the wilderness.

'And, as to the gossip columns, I'm sure they'd be much more interested in the scoop of seeing the Grand Duchess Honoria Maria Escalona being forcibly ejected from the offices of Sarova International—and I can just imagine some of the stories they might come up with to explain your expulsion.'

'Not so much of a Grand Duchess any more,' Ria admitted without thinking. 'Not so much of a duchess of any sort.'

'What?'

That brought him up sharp. Just for a second or two blank confusion clouded those amazing eyes and he tilted his head slightly to one side as a puzzled frown drew his brows together. The small, revealing moment caught on something in her heart and twisted painfully.

He had always done that when she had known him before. When they had been children together—well, she had been the child and he a lordly six years older. If he was confused or uncertain that frown had creased the space between his dark brows and his head would angle to the side...

'Lexei—please.' The name slipped from her before she could think. The familiar, affectionate name that she had once been able to use.

But she'd made a fatal mistake. She knew that as soon as the words had left her mouth and his reaction left her in no doubt at all that the one slip of her lips, in the hope of getting a tiny bit closer to him, had had the opposite effect.

His long body stiffened in rejection, that slight tilt of his head turned into a stiff-necked gesture of antagonism as his chin came up, angry, rejecting. His eyes flashed and his mouth tightened, pulling the muscles in his jaw into an uncompromising line.

'No,' he said, hard and rough. 'No. I will not listen to a word you say. Why should I when you and yours turned your back on my mother—on me—and left us to exile and disgrace? My mother *died* in that disgrace. It's not as if anything you have to say is a matter of life or death.'

'Oh, but...'

It could be... The words died on her tongue, burned away in the flare of fury he turned on her, seeming to scorch her skin so painfully.

This was not how she had planned it, but it was obvious that he wasn't prepared to let her lead up to things with a carefully prepared conversation. Hastily she grabbed at her handbag, snapping it open with hands made clumsy by nerves.

'This is for you...' she managed, holding out the sheet of paper she had folded so carefully at the start of her journey. The document she had checked was still there at least once every few minutes on her way here.

His eyes dropped to what she held, expression freezing

into marble stillness as he took in the crest at the head of the sheet of paper, the seal that marked it out for the important document it was.

'You know that your mother needed proof of the legality of her marriage,' she tried and got the briefest, most curt nod possible as his only response, his gaze still fixed on the document she held out.

It was like talking to a statue, he was so stiff, so unmoving, and she found that her tongue was stumbling over itself as she tried to get the words out. If only someone else could have been given this vital duty to carry out. But she had volunteered herself in spite of the fact that the ministers had viewed her with suspicion. A suspicion that was natural, after the way her father had behaved. But they didn't know the half of it. She had only just discovered the truth for herself and hadn't dared to reveal any of it to anyone else. Luckily, the ministers had been convinced that she was the most likely to be successful. Alexei would listen to her, they had said. And besides, with success meaning so much to her personally, to her family, she would be the strongest advocate at this time.

It was a strong irony that all the discipline, the training her father had imposed on her for his own ends, was now to be put to use to try to thwart those ends if she possibly could.

'And for that she needed evidence of the fact that the old king had given his permission for your father—as a member of the royal family—to marry all those years ago, when they first met.'

Why was she repeating all this? He knew every detail as much as she did. After all, it had been his life that had been blasted apart by the scandal that had resulted when it had seemed that his parents' marriage had been declared illegal. Alexei's father and mother had been separated, with him living with his mother in England until he was sixteen, and the fact that her husband was ill—dying of cancer—had brought his mother to Mecjoria in hope of a reconciliation. They hadn't had long and, during what time they had had, Alexei had found the old-fashioned and snobbish aristocracy difficult to deal with, particularly when they had regarded him and his mother as nothing more than commoners who didn't belong at court. His rebellious behaviour had created disapproval, brought him under the disapproving gaze of so many. And too soon, with his father dead, there had been no one to support his mother, or her son, when court conspiracy—a conspiracy Ria had just discovered to her horror of which her father had been an important part—had had her expelled, exiled from the country, taking her son with her.

Then there was her own part in all of it—her own guilty conscience, Ria acknowledged. That was an important part of why she had volunteered to come here today, to bring the news of the discovery of the document…and the rest.

'This is the evidence.'

At last he moved, reached out a hand and took the paper from her. But to her shock he simply glanced swiftly over the text then tossed it aside, dropping it on to his desk without a second glance.

'So?'

The single word seemed to strip all the moisture from her mouth, making her voice cracked and raw as she tried to answer him.

'Don't you see…?' Silly question. Of course he saw, he just wasn't reacting at all as she had expected, as she had been led to believe he would inevitably react. 'This is what you needed back then, this changes everything.

It means that your parents were legally married even in Mecjoria. It makes you legitimate.'

'And that makes me fit to have you come and visit me? Speak to me after all these years?'

The bitterness in his tone made her flinch. Even more so because she knew she deserved it. She'd flung that illegitimacy—that supposed illegitimacy—at him when he had asked for her help. She hadn't known the truth then, but she knew now that she'd done it partly out of hurt and anger too. Hurt and anger that he had turned away from her to become involved in a romantic entanglement with another girl.

A woman, Ria. She could hear his voice through the years. *She's a woman.*

And the implication was that *she* was still a child. Hurt and feeling rejected, she had been the perfect target for her father's story—what she knew now were her father's lies.

'It's not that…' Struggling with her memories, she had to force the words out. 'It's what's *right.*'

She knew how much he'd loathed the label 'bastard'. But more so how he'd hated the way that his mother had been treated because her marriage hadn't been considered legal. So much so that Ria had believed—hoped— that the news she had brought would change everything. She couldn't have been more wrong.

'Right?' he questioned cynically. 'From where I stand it's too little too late. The truth can't help my mother now. And personally I couldn't give a damn what they think of me in Mecjoria any more. But thank you for bringing it to me.'

His tone took the words to a meaning at the far opposite of genuine thankfulness.

There was much more to it than this. The proof of his legitimacy came with so many repercussions, but she had never expected this reaction. Or, rather, this lack of reaction.

'I'm sorry for the way I behaved...' she began, trying a different tack. One that earned her nothing but a cold stare.

'It was ten years ago.' He shrugged powerful shoulders in dismissal of her stumbling apology. 'A lot of water has passed under a lot of bridges since then. And none of it matters any more. I have made my own life and I want nothing more to do with a country that thought my mother and I were not good enough to live there.'

'But...'

There were so many details, so many facts, buzzing inside Ria's head but she didn't dare to let any of them out. Not yet. There was too much riding on them and this man was not prepared to listen to a word she said. If she put one foot wrong he would reject her—and her mission—completely. And she would never get a second chance.

'So now I'd appreciate it if you'd leave. Or I will call security and have you thrown out, and to hell with the paparazzi or the gossip columnists. In fact, perhaps it would be better that way. They could have a field day with what I could tell them.'

Was it a real or an empty threat? And did she dare take the risk of finding out? Not with things the way they were back home, with the country in turmoil, hopes for security and peace depending on her. On a personal level, she feared her mother would break down completely if anything more happened, and she would be back under her father's control herself if she failed. One whiff of scandal in the papers could be so terribly damaging that she shivered just to think of it. The only way she could achieve everything she'd set out to do was to get Alexei on her side—but that was beginning to look increasingly impossible.

'Honoria,' Alexei said dangerously and she didn't need the warning in his tone to have her looking nervously towards the door he still held wide open. The simple fact that he had used her full name was enough on its own. 'Duchess,' he added with a coldly mocking bow.

But she couldn't make her feet move. She couldn't leave. Not with so much unsaid.

CHAPTER TWO

It's not as if it's a matter of life or death, Alexei had declared, the scorn in his voice lashing at her cruelly. But it would be if the situation in Mecjoria wasn't resolved soon; if Ivan took over. The late King Felix might have been petty and mean but he was as nothing when compared to the tyrant who might inherit the throne from him. With a violent effort, Ria controlled the shiver of reaction that threatened her composure.

She hadn't seen Alexei for ten years, but she had had close contact with his distant cousin Ivan in that time. And hadn't enjoyed a moment of it. She'd watched Ivan grow from the sort of small boy who pulled wings off butterflies and kicked cats into a man whose volatile, mean-minded temper was usually only barely under control. He was aggressive, greedy, dangerous for the country—and now, she had learned to her horror, a danger to her personally as a result of her father's machinations. And the only man between them and that possibility was Alexei.

But she knew how much she was asking of him. Especially now, when she knew how he still felt about Mecjoria.

'Please listen!'

But his face was armoured against her, his eyes hooded, and she felt that every look she turned on him, every word she spoke, simply bounced off his thick skin like a pebble off an elephant's hide.

'Please?' he echoed sardonically, his mouth twisting on the word as he turned it into a cruelly derisory echoing of her tone. 'I didn't even realise that you knew that word. Please *what,* Sweetheart?'

'You don't want to know.'

Bleak honesty made her admit it. She could read it in his face, in the cruel opacity of those coal-black eyes. There wasn't the faintest sign of softening in his expression or any of the lines around his nose and mouth. How could he take a gentle word like *'sweetheart'* and turn it into something hateful and vile with just his tone?

'Oh, but I do,' Alexei drawled, folding his arms across his broad chest and lounging back against the wall, one foot hooked round the base of the door so as to keep it open and so making it plain that he was still waiting— expecting her to leave. 'I'd love to know just what you've come looking for.'

'Really?'

Unexpected hope kicked hard in her heart. Had she got this all wrong, read him completely the wrong way round?

'Really,' he echoed sardonically. 'It's fascinating to see the tables turned. Remember how I once asked you for just one thing?'

He'd asked her to help him, and his mother. Asked her to talk to her father, plead with him to at least let them have something to live on, some part of his father's vast fortune that the state had confiscated, leaving Alexei and his mother penniless as well as homeless. And not knowing the truth, not understanding the machinations of the plotters, or how sick his mother actually was, she had seen him as a threat and sided with her father.

'I made a mistake…' she managed. She'd known that

her father was ruthless, ambitious, but she had never really believed that he would lie through his teeth, that he would manipulate an innocent woman and her son.

For the good of the country, Honoria, he had said. And, seeing the outrage Alexei's wayward behaviour had created, she had believed him. Because she had trusted her father. Trusted him and believed in the values of upright behaviour, of loyalty to the crown that he'd insisted on. So she'd believed him when he'd told her how the scandal of Alexei's mother's 'affair' with one of the younger royal sons was creating problems of state. It was only now, years later, that she'd discovered how much further his deception had gone, and how it had involved her.

'What is it, *darling?*' Alexei taunted. 'Not enjoying this?'

She saw the gleam of cruel amusement in his eyes, the fiendish smile curling the corners of the beautiful mouth. Each of them spoke of cold contempt, but together they spelled a callous triumph at the thought of getting her exactly where he wanted her. She knew now that this man would delight in rejecting anything she said, if only to have his revenge on the family that he saw as the ringleaders of his downfall. And who could blame him?

But would he do the same for his country?

'It's no fun having to beg, is it? No fun having to crawl to someone you'd much rather die than even talk to.'

Once more that searing gaze raked over her from the top of her uncharacteristically controlled hair down to the neat, highly polished black shoes. It was a look that took her back ten years, forced her to remember how coldly he had regarded her before he had walked away and out of her life. For good, she had thought then.

'And I should know, angel—I've been there, remember? I've been exactly where you are now—begged, pleaded—and walked away with nothing.'

He might look indolently relaxed and at his ease as he lounged back against the wall, still with those strong arms crossed over the width of his chest, but in reality his position was the taut, expectant posture of a wily, knowing hunter, a predator that was poised, watching and waiting. He only needed his prey—her—to make one move and then he would pounce, hard and fast.

But still she had to try.

'You are wanted back in Mecjoria,' she blurted out in an uneven rush.

She could tell his response even before he opened his mouth. The way that long straight spine stiffened, the tightening of the beautiful lips, the way a muscle in his jaw jerked just once.

'You couldn't have said anything less likely to make me want to know more,' he drawled, dark and slow. 'But you could try to persuade me...'

She could try, but it would have no effect, his tone, his stony expression told her. And she didn't like the thought of just what sort of 'persuasion' could be in his mind. She wasn't prepared to give him that satisfaction.

Calling on every ounce of strength she possessed, stiffening her back, straightening her shoulders, she managed to lift her head high, force her green eyes to meet those icy black ones head-on.

'No thank you,' she managed, her tone pure ice.

Her father would have been proud of her for this at least. She was the Grand Duchess Honoria Maria at her very best. The only daughter of the Chancellor, faced by a troublesome member of the public. The trouble was that after all she had learned about her father's schemes, the way that he had seen her as a way to further his own power, she didn't want to be that woman any more. She had actually hoped that by coming here today she could free herself from the toxic inheritance that came with that title.

'You might get off on that sort of thing, but it certainly does nothing for me.'

If she had hoped that he would look at least a little crestfallen, a touch deflated, then she was doomed to disappointment. There might have been a tiny acknowledgement of her response in his eyes, a gleam that could have been a touch of admiration—or a hint of dark satisfaction from a man who had known all along just how she would respond.

She'd dug herself a hole without him needing to push her into it. But, for now, was discretion the better part of valour? She could let Alexei think that he had won this round at least but it was only one battle, not the whole war. There was too much at stake for that.

'Thank you for your time.'

She couldn't so much as turn a glance in his direction, even though she caught another wave of that citrus scent as he came closer, with the undertones of clean male skin that almost destroyed her hard-won courage. But even as she fought with her reactions he fired another comment at her. One that tightened a slackening resolve, and reminded her just how much the boy she had once known had changed.

'I wish that I could say it had been a pleasure,' he drawled cynically. 'But we both know that that would be a lie.'

'We certainly do,' Ria managed from between lips that felt as if they had turned to wood, they were so stiff and tight.

'So now you'll leave. Give my regards to your father,' Alexei tossed after her.

He couldn't have said anything that was more guaranteed to force her to stay. A battle, not the war, she reminded herself. She wasn't going to let this be the last of it. She couldn't.

He was going to let her go, Alexei told himself. In fact he would be glad to do so even if the thundering response that she had so unexpectedly woken in his body demanded otherwise. He wanted her to walk away, to take with her the remembrance of the family he had hoped to find, a life he had once tried to live, a girl he had once cared for.

'Lexei... Please...'

The echo of her voice, soft and shaken—or so he would have sworn—swirled in his thoughts in spite of his determination to clamp down on the memory, to refuse to let it take root there. Violently he shook his head to try and drive away the sound but it seemed to cling like dark smoke around his thoughts, bringing with it too many memories that he had thought he'd driven far away.

At first she had knocked him mentally off-balance with the news she had brought. The news he had been waiting to hear for so long—half a lifetime, it seemed. The document she had held out to him now lay on his desk, giving him the legitimacy, the position in Mecjoria he had wanted—that he had thought he wanted—but he didn't even spare it a second glance. It was too late. Far, far too late. His mother, to whom this had mattered so much, was dead, and he no longer gave a damn.

But something tugging at the back of his thoughts, an itch of something uncomfortable and unexpected, told him that that wasn't the real truth. There was more to this than just the delivery of that document.

'Not so much of Grand Duchess any more,' Ria had

said to him unexpectedly. *'Not so much of a duchess of any sort.'*

And that was when it struck him. There was something missing. *Someone* missing. Someone he should have noticed was not there from the first moment in the room but he had been so knocked off-balance that he hadn't registered anything beyond the fact that *Ria* was there in his office, waiting for him.

Where was the dark-suited bodyguard? The man who had the knack of blending into the background when necessary but who was alert and ready to move forward at any moment if their patron appeared to be in any difficulty?

There was no one with her now. There had been no one when he had arrived in this room to find her waiting for him. And there should have been.

What the hell was going on?

He couldn't be unaware of the present political situation in Mecjoria. There had been so many reports of marches on the streets, of protest meetings in the square of the capital. Ria's father, the Grand Duke Escalona, High Chancellor of the country, had been seen making impassioned speeches, ardent broadcasts, calling for calm—ordering the people to stay indoors, keep off the streets. But that had been before first the King and then the new heir to the throne had died so unexpectedly. Before the whole question of the succession had come under scrutiny with meetings and conferences and legal debates to call into question just what would happen next. He had paid it as little attention as it deserved in his own mind, but it had been impossible to ignore some of the headlines—like the ones that declared the country was on the brink of revolution.

It was his father's country after all. The place he should have called his home if he hadn't been forced out before he came to settle in any way. Without ever having a chance to get to know the father who had been missing from his life.

'*Lexei... Please...*'

He would have been all right if she hadn't used that name. If she hadn't—deliberately he was sure—turned on him the once warm, affectionate name she had used back in the gentler, more innocent days when he had thought that they were friends. And so whirled him back into memories of a past he'd wanted to forget.

'All right, I'm intrigued.' And that was nothing less than the truth. 'You clearly have something more to say. So—you have ten minutes. Ten minutes in which to tell me the truth about why you're here. What had you appearing in my office unannounced, declaring you were no longer a grand duchess. Is that the truth?'

It seemed it had to be—or at least that something in what he had said had really got to her. She had reacted to his words as if she had been stung violently. Her head had gone back, her green eyes widening in reaction at something. Her soft rose-tinted mouth had opened slightly on a gasp of shock.

A shock that ricocheted through his own frame as a hard kick of some totally primitive sexual hunger hit home low down in his body. Those widened eyes looked stunning and dark against the translucent delicacy of her skin, and that mouth was pure temptation in its half-open state.

His little friend Ria had grown up into a beautiful woman and that unthinkingly primitive reaction to the fact jolted him out of any hope of seeing her just as the girl she had once been. Suddenly he was unable to look at her in any way other than as a man looks at a woman he desires. His own mouth hungered to take those softly parted lips, to taste her, feel her yield to him, surrendering, opening… His heart thudded hard and deep in his chest, making him need to catch his breath as his body tightened in pagan hunger.

'You don't believe me?' she questioned and the uncharacteristic hesitation on the word twisted something deep inside him, something he no longer thought existed. Something that it seemed that only this woman could drag up from deep inside him. A woman who had once been the only friend he thought he had and who now had been reincarnated as a woman who heated his blood and turned him on more than he could recall anyone doing in the past months—the past years.

It was like coming awake again after being dead to his senses for years—and it hurt.

'It's not that I don't believe you.'

The fight he was having to control the sensual impulses of his body showed in his voice and he saw the worried, apprehensive look she shot him sideways from under the long, lush lashes. She clearly didn't know which way to take him, a thought that sent a heated rush of satisfaction through his blood. He wanted her off-balance, on edge. That way she might let slip more than her carefully cultivated, court training would allow her.

'Merely that I see no reason why you or any member of your family would renounce the royal title that has meant so much to you.'

'We didn't renounce it. It was renounced for us.'

A frown snapped Alexei's black brows together sharply as he focussed even more intently on her face, trying to read what was there.

'And just what does that mean? I've heard nothing of this.'

How had he missed such an important event? The people he had employed to watch what was happening in

Mecjoria should have been aware of it. They should have investigated and reported back to him.

'It's been kept very quiet—at the moment my father is officially "resting" to recover from illness.'

'When the reality is?'

'That he's under arrest.'

Her voice caught on the word, a soft little hiccup that did disturbing things to the tension at his groin, tightening it a notch or two uncomfortably.

'And is now in the state prison.'

That was the last thing he'd expected and it shocked some of the desire from him, making his head swim slightly at the rush of blood from one part of his body to his head.

'On what charge?' he demanded sharply.

'No charge.' She shook her head, sending her dark hair flying. 'Not as yet—that—that all depends on how things work out.'

'So what the hell did he do wrong?' Gregor had always seemed such a canny player. Someone who knew how best to feather his own nest. So had he got too greedy, made some mistake?

'He—chose the wrong side in the recent inheritance battle. For the throne.'

So that was what was behind this. Alexei might never want to set foot in Mecjoria ever again, but he couldn't be unaware—no one could be unaware—of the struggle that had gone on over the inheritance of the throne once old King Leopold had died. First Leopold's son Marcus had inherited, but only briefly. A savage heart attack had killed him barely months into his reign. Because he had died childless, his nephew Felix should have inherited the crown, but his wild way of life had been his undoing, so that he had died in a high-speed car crash before he had even ascended to the throne. Now there were several factions warring over just who was the legal heir to follow Felix.

'And then when Felix died… My father is currently seen as an enemy—as a threat to the throne.'

She wasn't telling the full truth, Alexei realised. There was something she was holding back, he was sure of it. Something that clouded those amazing eyes, tightened the muscles around her delicate jawline, pulling the pretty mouth tight, though there was no mistaking the quiver of those softly sensual lips.

Lips that he wished to hell he could taste, feel that trembling softness under his own mouth, plunder the moist interior…

'It will all work out in the end.'

Once again his own burning inner feelings made the words sound abrupt, dismissive, and he saw her blink slowly, withdrawing from him. Her head came up, that smooth chin lifting in defiance as she met his stare face-on.

'You can promise that, can you?' Ria asked, her tone appallingly cynical.

And where her unexpected weakness hadn't beaten him now, shockingly, her boldness did. There was a new spark in her eyes, fresh colour in her cheeks. She was once more the proud Grand Duchess Honoria and not the strangely defeated girl who had reached out to something he had thought was long dead inside him. *This* Ria was a challenge; a challenge he welcomed. The sound of his blood was like a roar inside his head, the heated race of his pulse burning along every vein. He had never wanted a woman so much as he wanted her now, and the need was like an ache in every nerve.

'How would you know? You were the one who turned

your back on Mecjoria—haven't even been back once in ten years.'

'Not turned my back,' Alexei growled. 'We weren't given a chance to stay. In fact it was made plain that we were not wanted.'

And who had been behind that? Her father—the very same man who was now, according to her story, locked in a prison cell. Did she expect him to feel sorry for him? To give a damn what might happen to the monster who hadn't even waited to allow him and his mother time to mourn their loss, or even to attend the state funeral, before he had had them escorted to the airport and put on the first plane out of the country?

First making sure that every penny of his father's fortune, every jewel, every tiny personal inheritance, had been taken from them, leaving them with little but the clothes they stood up in, not even the most basic allowance to see them into their new life in exile. Worst of all, Gregor had taken their name from them. The name his mother had been entitled to, and with it her honour, the legality of her marriage into the royal house of Mecjoria. He must have done it deliberately, hiding away the document that showed the old king's permission. The document that Ria had been commissioned to bring here so unexpectedly—because it now suited her father. Was it any wonder that he loathed the man—that he would do anything to bring him down?

But it seemed that Gregor had managed that all on his own.

'And I don't have to be in the country to know what is going on.'

'The papers don't report everything. And certainly not always accurately.'

Something new had clouded those clear eyes and

turned her expression into an intriguing mixture of defiance and uncertainty. There was just the tiniest sheen of moisture under one eye, where a trace of an unexpected tear had escaped the determined control she had been trying to impose on it and slipped out on to her lashes.

Unable to resist the impulse, he reached out and touched her face, letting his fingers rest lightly on the fine skin along the high, slanting cheekbone, wiping away that touch of moisture. The warmth and softness of the contact made his nerves burn, sending stinging arrows of response down into his body. He wanted so much more and yet he wanted to keep things just as they were—for now. It was a struggle not to do more, not to curve his hand around her cheek, cup that defiant little chin against his palm, lift her face towards his so that he could capture her mouth...

And that would ruin things completely. She would react like a scalded cat, he had no doubt. All that silent defiance would return in full force, and she'd swing away from him, repulsing the gesture with a rough shake of her head. She was still too tense, too on edge. But like any nervous cat, with a few moments' careful attention—perhaps a soothing stroke or two—she would soon settle down.

So for now it was enough to watch the storm of emotions that swept over her face. The response that turned those citrine eyes smoky, that darkened and deepened the black of her pupils, making them spread like the flow of ink until they covered almost all of her irises. The way that her mouth opened again to show the tips of small white teeth was a temptation that kicked at his libido, making it hungrier than ever. The clamour in his body urged him to act, to make his move now, when she was at her weakest, but for a little while at least he was enjoying imposing restraint on himself, letting the sensual hunger build—anticipating what might come later—and watching the effect his behaviour had on her.

'So tell me the rest.'

She didn't know if she could go through with this. Ria struggled to find some of the certainty, the conviction of doing the right thing, that had buoyed her up on her journey here, held her in the room in spite of the frantic thudding of her heart. So much depended on what she said now and the possible repercussions of her failure, personal and political, were almost impossible to imagine. The image of her mother, too pale, far too thin, drifting through life like a wraith, with no appetite, no interest in anything slid into her mind. Her days were haunted by fears, her nights plagued by terrifying nightmares.

Her father was the cause of those nightmares. Since the night that the state police had come to arrest him, taking him away in handcuffs, they had never seen him for a moment. But they knew where he was. The state prison doors had slammed closed on him and, unless Ria could find some way of helping him, then behind those locked doors was where he was going to stay. She had wanted to help him—wanted to return him to her mother—and it had been because she had been looking for some way to do that that she had found the hidden documents, the ones that proved Alexei's legitimacy and the others that had revealed the whole truth about what had been going on.

The full, appalling truth.

CHAPTER THREE

IT WAS WHAT she had come here for, Ria reminded herself. To tell him the story that had not yet leaked into the papers. The full details of the archaic inheritance laws that had come into play in the country since the unexpected death of the man they had believed to be the heir to the throne. But that would also mean telling him how those laws involved him, and his reaction just a moment before had made it plain that he harboured no warmth towards the country that had once been his home.

But when he had touched her—the way he still touched her—just that one tiny contact seemed to have broken through the careful, deliberate barriers she had built around herself. It was so long since she had felt that someone sympathised; that someone might be on her side. And the fact that it was someone as strong and forceful—and devastating—as this particular man, the man who had once been a special friend to her, stripped away several much-needed protective layers of skin, leaving her raw and disturbingly vulnerable.

He was so close she couldn't actually judge his expression without lifting her head, tilting it back just a little. And that movement brought her eyes up to clash with his. Suddenly even breathing naturally was impossible as their gazes locked, the darkness and intensity of his stare closing her throat in the space of a single uneven heartbeat.

In that moment everything that had happened in the past months rushed up to swamp her mind, taking with it any hope of rational thought. Except that right now she needed him. Needed the friend he had once been. So much about him might have changed: that hard-boned face had thinned, toughened into that of a stunningly mature male in his sexual prime; those eyes might now be five inches above hers where once they had been so much closer to her own... But they were still the eyes of the friend she had known. Still the eyes of the one person she had felt she could confide in and get a sympathetic hearing.

They were the eyes she had once let herself dream of seeing warm with more than just the easy light of friendship. And the memory of how in the past she had fallen asleep and into dreams of them being so much more than friends twisted in her heart with the bitterness of loss.

'Tell me everything.'

'You don't really want that,' she flung at him, gulping in air so that she could loosen her throat.

'No? Try me.'

Challenge blended with something else in his tone. And it was that something else that made her heart jerk, her breath catch.

Was it possible that he really did want to know? That he might help her? Memories of their past friendship surfaced once again, tugging at her feelings. She was so lonely, so dragged down by it all, so tired of coping with everything on her own. So wretched at the thought of what the future might bring. And here was this man who had once been the boy she adored, the friend who had let her offload her troubles on to his shoulders—shoulders that even then had seemed broad enough to take on the world. They were so much broader, so much stronger now.

Tell me everything, he'd said, and as he spoke the hand that rested against her face moved slightly, the pressure of his fingers softening, his palm curving so that it lay over her cheek, warm and hard and yet gentle all at the same time.

'*The truth,* Ria,' he said and the sound of her name on his lips was her weakness, her undoing.

Unable to stop herself, she turned her face into his hold, inhaling the scent of his skin, pursing her lips to press a small, soft kiss against the warmth of his palm.

Instantly everything changed. Her heart seemed to stop, her breathing stilled. The clean, musky aroma of his body was all around her, the taste of his flesh tangy on her tongue. It was like taking a sip of a fine, smoky brandy, one that intoxicated in a moment, sending fizzing bubbles of electricity along every nerve.

She wanted more. Needed to deepen the contact. Needed it like never before.

The boy who had been her friend had never made her feel like this; never made her pulse race so fast and heavy, her head spin so wildly. In all her adolescent dreams she had never known this feeling of awareness, of hunger. A pulsing, heated adult hunger that grew and sharpened as he moved his hold on her, taking her chin and lifting it so that their eyes clashed and scorched. Something blazed in these black depths, creating a golden glow that had more heat than an inferno and yet was almost—*almost*—under control.

'Ria...' he said again, his tone very different this time, his voice roughening at the edges. He had moved closer somehow, without her noticing, and the warmth of his breath on her skin as he spoke her name sent heated shiv-

ers running down her spine, making her toes curl inside
her neat, polished shoes.

'Alex…'

But speaking had been a mistake. It made her mouth
move against his skin, brought that powerfully sensual
taste onto her tongue once again, so that she swallowed
convulsively, taking the essence of him into herself in an
echo of a much more intimate blending. Immediately it
was as if a lighted match had been set to desert-dry brush-
wood. As if the tiny flicker that had been smouldering
deep inside from the moment that she had come face to
face with him again in his office had suddenly burst into
wild and uncontrollable flame, the force of it moving her
forward sharply, close up against him.

She heard his breath hiss in between his teeth in an
uncontrolled response that both shocked and thrilled her.
The thought that he felt as she did, so much that he was
unable to hide his response from her, made her head spin.
She could hardly believe that it could be possible, but there
was no denying the evidence of the way that his grip tightened on her chin, hard fingers digging into her skin as he
lifted her face towards his with a roughness that betrayed
the urgency of his feelings.

'Alex…' she tried again, trying to follow the safe, the
sensible path and persuade him to stop, but realising as
she heard her own voice that she was doing exactly the
opposite. The quaver on his name sounded so much more
like shaken encouragement.

But a moment later it didn't matter what she said or how
she said it. The truth was that she was incapable of any
further speech as Alexei's dark head swooped down, his
mouth capturing hers in a savage kiss. Hard lips crushed
hers, bringing them open to the invasion of his tongue in
an intimate dance that made her knees weaken so that she

swayed against him, her body melting soft and yielding against the hardness of his.

She heard him mutter something dark and deep in his throat and the next moment she was swung round and up into his arms. Half-walked, half-carried across the room, his mouth never leaving hers, until she was hard up against the wall, its support cold and hard against her back. Both thrilled and shocked by his unexpected response, she shivered under the impact of his powerful form on her, the heat and hardness of him crushed against the cradle of her pelvis. If she had needed any further evidence of the fact that his blood was burning as hot as hers, then it was there in the swollen, powerful erection that was crushed between them.

His mouth was plundering hers, his tongue sweeping into the innermost corners, tasting her, tormenting her. The heated pressure of his hands matched the intimate invasion of his mouth, hot, hard palms skimming over her body, burning through the flowered cotton of her dress, curving over the swell of her hips, cupping her buttocks to pull her closer to him. Ria's blood pounded at her temples, along every nerve. Her breasts prickled and tightened in stinging response, nipples pressing against the soft lace of her bra, hungry for the feel of those wickedly enticing fingers against her flesh.

Unable to stop herself, she nipped sharply at his lower lip, catching it between her teeth and taking his gasp of response into her mouth with the taste of him clear and wild against her lips. Pushed into penitence by his reaction, she let her tongue slide over the damaged skin, soothing the small pressure wounds her teeth had inflicted and sucking the fullness of it to ease away any soreness. But the low growl she heard deep in his throat told her that his reaction had not been one of discomfort. Instead he was encouraging her to take further liberties, crushing her hard against him and letting his hands wander freely over her yearning body.

'Hell, but you're beautiful...'

He muttered the words against her arching throat, his breath warm against her flesh, and she could hardly believe that she was hearing them. Had he truly said beautiful? Was it possible that the man the gossip columns labelled the playboy prince, who had his pick of the sexiest women in the world—socialites, models, actresses—could think her so attractive? Memories of the adolescent dreams she had once indulged in, the yearning crush she had felt for this man surfaced all over again, reminding her of how much she would have given to hear those words back then, years ago. Then all he had ever shown her was a kind, but rather offhand friendship that was light-years away from this carnal hunger that seemed to grip them now.

'Who would have thought that you would grow up like this?'

'It—it's been a long time,' Ria managed to choke out, her throat dry with tension and need. 'I missed...'

But a sudden rush of self-preservation had her catching up the words in shock, clamping her mouth tight shut against what she had almost revealed. The heady rush of sensuality had driven common sense so far from her mind but she needed to grab it back now—and quickly. Alexei was no longer even her friend. He was the man who held her future and that of her country in his hands, even if he didn't know it yet.

In the strong, sensual hands that had been creating such electric pulses of pleasure in her body only a moment before. Pulses she wanted to feel more of. That made her whole body ache with need. But she must deny herself such caresses even though her whole body screamed in protest at the thought of stopping now, here, like this, when every nerve had suddenly come alive and awake in a whole new way. She had to remember why she was here.

'You—you've been missed,' she managed, though her voice shook on the words, betraying the effort she was making to get them out. And then, suddenly aware of how that might sound—that he could interpret it as meaning she was telling him just how much *she* had missed him— she rushed on. 'You've been missed in Mecjoria.'

The sound of that name brought exactly the reaction she feared. She felt the new tension in the long body pressed against hers as he stilled, withdrawing from her immediately, his hands freezing, denying her the shivers of pleasure that had radiated out from his touch.

'I doubt that very much,' he muttered, his voice rough and harsh so that it scraped over her rawly exposed nerves. 'I don't think that could ever be true.'

'Oh, but it is!' Ria protested, forcing herself to go on because this was what she had come here for after all. 'You're missed in Mecjoria—and wanted and needed there.'

'Needed?'

Her heart sank as he pushed himself away from her to stand looking down into her face with icy onyx eyes, all fire, all warmth fading from them in the space of a heartbeat. She had done what she needed to do, turned things back on to the real reason why she was here, so that at last she could tell him just why she had come to find him. But she felt lost and alone, her body suddenly cold and bereft without the heat and power of his surrounding it; her skin, her breasts, her lips cooling sharply as the imprint of his whipcord strength evaporated into the cool of the afternoon air.

She'd lost him again. That much was obvious from one swift glance at his face, seeing the way it had closed off against her, black eyes opaque and expressionless, revealing nothing. His only movement was when his hand went to his throat, tugging at the tie around his neck as if it was choking him. He pulled it loose, flicked open the top button on his shirt, then another, as if just one was not enough. And the restless movement was enough to draw her eyes, make her watch in stunned fascination.

No, that was a mistake—a major mistake. Looking into those deep-set black eyes, she suddenly saw a new light, a darkly burning, disturbing light in their depths, and it warned that there was more to this than anything she might have anticipated already. Memory swung her back to the scene of just moments before. Then, pinned up against the wall with his hands hot on her, she had known exactly what he wanted. And she had been dangerously close to giving it to him, with no thought of her own sanity or safety. Her body still tingled with the aftershocks of that encounter, the taste of him still lingered on her mouth. If she licked her lips she revived the sensation, almost as if he had just kissed her again. And oh, dear heaven, but she wanted him to kiss her again.

'There is no one there who would miss me and as for anyone who might *want* me for any reason whatsoever...'

'Oh, but you're wrong there. You really are.'

But how did she convince him of that? If there was anything that brought home to her how difficult her task was then this office, this building, was it. She didn't need to be told how much Alexei had made his new life here in England. More than a new life, his fortune, his *home*. And it was plain from the way he spoke of Mecjoria that his father's country meant nothing to him. Did she even have the right to ask him to give this up?

She didn't know. But the one thing she was sure of was that she didn't have the right to keep it from him. The decision, whatever it was, had to be his.

'I'll make it easy for you, shall I?' Alexei drawled cynically. 'Twice now you have told me that I am wanted—and needed—in Mecjoria. You have to be lying.'

'No lie. Really.'

'You expect me to believe that I am needed in the country that rejected me as not fit to be even the smallest part of the royal family? Needed by the place that has disowned and ignored me for the past ten years?'

The only response Ria could manage was a sharp, swift nod of her head. She couldn't persuade her voice to work on anything else.

'Then you'll have to explain. Needed as what?'

'As...'

Twice Ria opened her mouth to try to get the words out. Twice she failed, and it was only when Alexei turned his narrow-eyed glare on her and muttered her name as if in threat that she forced herself to speak, bringing it out in a rush.

'As—as their king. You're needed to take the throne of Mecjoria now that Felix is dead.'

CHAPTER FOUR

As THEIR KING.

The words hit like a blow to the head, making Alexei's thoughts reel. Had he heard right?

You're needed to take the throne of Mecjoria now that Felix is dead.

Whatever else he had expected, it had not been that. She had made it plain that she and her family had suffered some strong reversal of their fortunes in the upheaval that had followed the struggles over the inheritance of the Mecjorian crown. She had come here to ask for help, that much was obvious. Softening him up by producing the proof of his legitimacy first. Perhaps to play on the fact that they had once been friends in order to get him to use his fortune to help, rescue her family. Why else would she be here?

Why else would she have responded to his kisses as she had?

Because even as he had felt her mouth opening under his, the soft curves of her body melting against him, he had known that she was only doing this for her own private reasons.

Known it and hadn't cared. He had let her lead him on in that way because he'd wanted it. No woman had excited him, aroused him so much with a single kiss. And there

had been plenty of women. His reputation as a playboy
had been well earned, and he had had a lot of fun earning it. At least at the beginning. It was only after Mariette—and Belle—that everything had changed. His mind
flinched away from the memory but there was no getting
away from the after-effects of that terrible day. His ap-
petites had become jaded; his senses numbed. Nothing
seemed to touch him like before. There was no longer the
thrill of the chase.

Not that he had to do any chasing. Women practically
threw themselves at him and he could have his pick of any
of them simply by saying the right word, turning a prac-
tised smile in their direction. He was under no illusions; he
knew it was his position and wealth that was such a strong
part of the attraction. That and the bad-boy reputation that
haunted him like a dark shadow. So many women wanted
to be the one who tamed him. But not one of them had
ever stood a chance. He had enjoyed them, shared their
beds, sometimes finding the oblivion he sought in their
arms. But not one of them had ever heated his blood, set
his pulse racing in burning hunger as this one kiss from
the former friend he had once known as a young girl, but
who had grown into a stunningly sexual woman.

A woman who, like so many others, had been prepared to use that sexuality to persuade him to give her
what she wanted.

But this…

'That's one hell of a bad joke!' He tossed the words
at her, saw her flinch from the harshness of his tone and
didn't care.

But then something about the way she looked, a widening of those amazing eyes, the sight of white, sharp
teeth digging into the rose-tinted softness of her lower

lip caught him up short and made him look again, more
closely this time. There was more to this than he believed.

'It was a joke, wasn't it?'

A bad, black-humorous joke. One meant to stick a knife
in between his ribs with the reminder of just how his father's homeland could never, ever be home to him again.
Even if he was the legitimate son of one of their royal family. Disbelief was like an itch in his blood, making him
want to pace around the room. Only the determination
not to show the way she had rocked his sense of reality
kept him still, one hand on the big, carved mantelpiece,
the other tightly clenched into a fist inside the pocket of
his trousers.

'A very bad joke...*no*...?'

She had shaken her head as he spoke, sending the auburn mane of her hair flying around her face. But it still
couldn't conceal the way she had lost even more colour,
her skin looking like putty, shocking in contrast to the
wide darkness of her eyes and the way that the blush of
colour flooded to where she had bitten into her lip again.

'No joke—' she stammered, low and uneven. 'It's not
something I'd ever joke about.'

How she wished he would show some sort of reaction,
Ria told herself. His stillness and the intent, fixed glare
were becoming seriously oppressive.

'But there's no way you can be telling the truth. How
would your father benefit from this?'

'My—my father?'

It would have the opposite effect, if only he knew. Her
father wouldn't benefit from this, rather he would gain
so much more from the back-up plan that would fall into
place if Alexei refused the request she had come to him
with. But she had promised herself that she would not tell
Alexei that; that she would never use the dark reality of

her own situation to try to persuade him into the decision she wanted—needed. Her family had committed enough crimes against his in the past. It was going to stop here, no matter what the result.

But she had hesitated too long. That, and her stammering response, had given her away.

'Your father must hope to get exactly what he wants from this.' It was a flat, cruel statement. 'Why else would he send you here?'

How did he manage to stay so still, so stiff, his eyes dark gleaming pools of contempt? He looked like a jewel-eyed cobra, silent, unmoving, just waiting for the moment to strike.

'My father wasn't the one who sent me, but obviously whatever you decide will affect him. And everyone in Mecjoria.'

'And I should care about that because…?'

'Because if you don't then the whole country will fall into chaos. There will be civil unrest, perhaps even revolution. People will be hurt—killed—they'll lose everything.'

The desperation she felt now sounded in her voice but it was clear that it had no effect on that flinty-eyed stare, the cold set of his hard jaw.

'And if you don't take the throne, the only other person who can is Ivan.'

That hit home to him.

She saw his head go back, eyes narrowing sharply at that, and knew the impact her words had had. Only very distantly related, Alexei and Ivan Kolosky had always detested each other. In fact Ivan had once been one of the ringleaders in making Alexei's life hell as he tried to adjust to life at the Mecjorian court, and they had once bonded together against this cousin several times removed who now was the only other possible heir to the Mecjo-rian throne.

With one proviso. One that affected her personally in a way that made her stomach curdle just to think of it. And she certainly didn't want Alexei to know of it or she would be putting extra power into his hands. Power she had no idea just how he would use.

'How would he be next in line to the succession?'

'There are ancient laws about the possible heirs. With both the old king and Felix gone, they have to look fur-ther afield. And with no one who's a direct descendant left then the net spreads wider—to you.'

'And to Ivan.'

It was throwaway, totally dismissive, and it warned her of just what was coming. The indifferent shrug of his shoulders only confirmed it.

'So, problem solved. You already have an heir—one who will want the throne much more than I ever would. You wouldn't even need to prove his legitimacy.'

The bitterness that twisted on his tongue made her wince in discomfort.

'But Ivan isn't the first in line. It's only if you refuse the crown that he has a claim.' Or if she played her own part in his succession as her father wanted. The knots in her stomach tightened painfully at the thought. 'And we can't let him take the crown!'

That had him turning a narrow-eyed stare on her shocked and worried face. It was so coldly, bleakly as-sessing that it made her shift uncomfortably where she stood. She was afraid that he would see her own fears in her expression and know that that gave him an advantage to hold over her.

'We?' he queried cynically. 'Since when was there any "we" involved in this?'

'You have to consider Mecjoria.'

'I do? I think you'll find that I don't have to do anything—or have anything to do with a country that was never a home to me.'

'But you must know all about the eruminium…the mineral that has been discovered in the mountains,' she explained when he made no response other than a sardonic lift of one black brow that cynically questioned her assertion. 'You'll know that it's being mined…'

'An excellent source of wealth for my cousin,' Alexei drawled, lounging back indolently against the wall in a way that expressed his total indifference to everything she said.

'But it's what it could be used for—eruminium can be used to make weapons almost as dangerous as an atomic bomb. Ivan won't care what it's used for—he'll sell the mining rights to anyone for the highest offer.'

Something flickered in the depths of those stunning eyes. But she couldn't be sure whether it was the sort of reaction that might help her or one that displayed exactly the opposite.

'And you actually concede that I might not do just the same?'

'I have to hope that you wouldn't.'

Ria no longer cared if her near-panic showed in her voice. Nothing about this meeting was going as she had thought—as she had hoped. Everyone had told her that all she had to do was to talk with Alexei, get him to listen to reason. He would grab at the position, the crown, they had assured her. How could he not when it offered him the wealth and power he must want?

Anyone who thought that had never seen the man Alexei had become, she told herself, looking at the elegantly lean and dangerous figure opposite her. It was

obvious that Alexei Sarova had everything he wanted
right here.

And, worst of all, was any suggestion that his taking
the crown would do anything to help her, as her father's
daughter, would just provide the death blow to any hope
of persuading him to do so. The hatred that burned bone-
deep was not going to be easily tossed aside.

'Only hope?' His question seemed to chip away layers of her protective shell, leaving gaping holes where
she most needed a shield. 'Well, what else should I have
expected?'

There was something that burned in those deep, black
eyes that challenged and scoured across her nerves all in
the same moment. But there was something else mixed
in there too, something she couldn't begin to interpret.

'I can't say for sure, can I? After all, I don't know you.'

'No,' Alexei drawled, another challenge, darker than
ever. 'You don't.'

'But I do know that if the problem of the succession
isn't solved soon then the whole country will fall into
chaos—possibly even revolution. You have to see that.'

'And I see that your father will find it very uncomfortable if that happens. But I don't understand why I need to
have any part in helping to deal with it. Your father betrayed mine—his memory—by claiming that his marriage
to my mother had never been legal. That was when he
wanted someone else to be on the throne—and for himself to have the strongest influence possible.'

The words seemed to strip away a much-needed protective layer of skin, leaving Ria feeling raw and painfully
exposed. Deep inside she knew she couldn't defend her
father from Alexei's accusations, and the truth was that
she didn't want to. In fact, she could add more to the list
if she had the chance.

'He destroyed my mother, took everything she had and threw her out of her home, the country.'

And her son with her, Ria acknowledged to herself, wincing inwardly at the cruelly sharp twist at her heart that the memory brought with it. Like everyone else, she'd believed her father's claims. She'd believed that he was loyal to the crown and to the country. She'd trusted him on that, only to find that all the time he had just been feathering his own nest, and planning on using her as his ace card if he could. But that had been before she had discovered that Gregor had held the document of permission all the time. That he had hidden it in order to get Alexei and his mother away from the court. Only now did she realise exactly why.

'But you've done fine for yourself since then.'

'Fine?'

One dark brow lifted in cynical mockery as he echoed her tone with deliberate accuracy.

'If you mean working every hour God sends to earn enough to support my mother and keep her in the way that she needed, give her some comfort and enjoyment when she was desperately ill, then yes, we've done "fine". But that in no way excuses your father for what he has done or puts me under any obligation at all to help him with anything.'

'No—no you're not,' she admitted. 'But don't you think that you might have played some part in what had driven him to push you into exile and kept you there afterwards?'

'And what exactly do you mean by that?'

The silence that greeted her question was appalling, dark and dangerous, bringing her up sharp against what she had said. What she had risked.

Oh, dear heaven, she had really opened her mouth and put both feet right in it there! All she had meant was that it had been his own irresponsible behaviour, the wildness of his ways, that had contributed to her father's reaction against him and his family. But now she had opened a very ugly can of worms, one she could never put the lid back on ever again. Alexei's behaviour at court had been one thing. There had been another, darker scandal that had cast a black shadow over his existence once he had settled in England.

'No—I'm sorry. Obviously...'

'Obviously?' Alexei echoed cynically. 'Obviously you think you know the answer to your question so why ask it?'

'I didn't mean to rake over the past.'

'You would be wise not to—not if you want me to do anything to help your father, because I'll see him in hell first.'

And that cold-blooded declaration was just too much. It wrenched the top off her control, taking her temper with it.

'Well, you'll be right there with him—won't you?' she flung at him. 'After all, what has my father done that compares with letting his baby die?'

It was as if the whole room had frozen over. As if the air had turned to ice, burning in her lungs and making it impossible to breathe. The cold was like a mist before her eyes but even with the swirling haze she could still see the blaze of his eyes, searing through the blurring clouds and scouring over her skin like some brutal laser.

'What indeed?'

She'd gone too far, said too much, and put herself in danger by doing so. Not physical danger because, no matter how darkly furious she knew that Alexei was, she also had a fiercely stubborn conviction that there was no way he would hurt her.

But mentally...that was another matter entirely. And

just the thought of it had her taking several hurried and shaken steps backwards, away from him, putting the width of the polished wooden desk between them for her own safety.

'I wouldn't be too sure of that.' The image of the jewel-eyed serpent was back in Ria's mind as she heard the vicious hiss of his words, felt the flicking sting of their poison. 'There are more ways than one to destroy a child's life.'

That brought her up sharply, blinking in shock and incomprehension as she stared into his dark shuttered face, trying to work out just what he meant. Had he known— or at the very least suspected—just what her father had planned? Was that why he had always been so aggressively hostile to the older man back in Mecjoria, so defiant, rejecting everything the Chancellor had tried to teach him? It was nothing but oppression, bullying, he had declared, and she had always come back with the belief that her father was doing it for their own good, and for the image of the country. At least that was how she had seen it at the time. Now, recognising the side of her father that had shown itself more recently, she was forced to see it in such a very different light, and the sense of betrayal was like acid in her mouth. But had Alexei, with the advantage of extra years, been able to interpret things much more accurately?

Because how could she deny the relevance his words had for her now, coming so close to the secret she had vowed she would keep from him at all costs?

'I didn't mean to rake over the past,' she said hesitantly, trying for appeasement.

'But nevertheless you have done just that.'

Black eyes blazed against skin drawn white across his slashing cheekbones and he slung the words at her like pellets of ice, each one seeming to hit hard and cold on her unprotected skin so that she flinched back, away from them.

'I'm sorry,' she tried but the icy flash of his eyes shrivelled the words on her tongue.

'Why apologise? Doesn't everyone know that I was once a useless, irresponsible drunk? The type of man who left my child alone while I went on a bender? Who drank myself into a stupor so that I didn't even know that my baby daughter had died in her cot?'

'Oh, don't!'

Her hands came up before her sharply in a gesture of defence. She didn't understand why it hurt so much just to hear the words. She'd known about it after all—everyone had. The scandal had exploded into the papers like an atom bomb, shattering lives, destroying what little reputation Alexei might still have had. Most of all it had ripped apart any hope she had clung on to that he might still be the boy she had loved so much—the friend who had once been her support and strength through a difficult, lonely childhood. It had certainly kept her from trying to contact him again when she had been tempted to do just that.

'Don't what?' he parried harshly. 'Don't acknowledge the truth?'

CHAPTER FIVE

HE'D BEEN HOLDING it together until she'd said that, Alexei acknowledged. Until she'd ripped away the protective wall he had built between himself and the dark remembrance of the past. And now the red mist of aching memory had seeped out and flooded his brain, making it impossible to think or to speak rationally.

Belle. One tiny little girl had changed his life and made him pull himself up, haul himself back from the edge of the precipice he had been rushing towards. But not soon enough. He had failed Belle, failed his daughter, and her death would always be on his conscience.

Looking into Ria's face, he could almost swear that he could see the sheen of moisture on those beautiful eyes and found that some inner of stab of jealousy actually twisted deep in his guts. He had never been able to weep for Belle, never been able to fully mourn her loss. He had been too busy trying to deal with the fallout from that tragedy.

But Ria… How could she have tears for a child she had never known, for a baby she had no connection to? He envied her her ease of response, the uncomplicated emotion.

'Why should I deny the facts when the world and his wife know what happened?' he demanded. 'And no one would believe a word that's different.'

'What possible different interpretation could there be?'

Was that what she was looking for? Hoping for? The questions thundered inside Ria's head, shocking her with their force, the bruising power of the need it startled into wakefulness. Was this what she wanted? That he could provide a different explanation for the terrible events of three years before? That he could explain it all away, say it had never happened—or at least that it had never been the way it had been reported? Was this why it tore at her so much, pulling a need she hadn't realised existed out of her heart and forcing her to face it head-on?

If that was it, then she was doomed to disappointment. She knew it as soon as she saw the way his face changed again, the bitter sneer that twisted his beautiful mouth, distorting its sensual softness.

'None, of course,' he drawled so softly that she almost missed it. 'That is unless you can tell me that you believe it could have been any other way. Can you do that, hmm, sweetheart?'

He went even more on to the attack, driving the savage stiletto blade of his cruelty deeper into her heart. And it was all the more devastating because it was still spoken in that dangerously gentle tone.

'Can you find a way to change the past so that the devil is transformed into an angel? A fallen angel, granted, but not the fiend incarnate that the world sees?'

Could she? Her mouth opened but no sound came out because there was no thought inside her head she could voice but the knowledge that what he spoke was the bitter, black truth.

'No...'

'No.'

The corners of his mouth curled up into a smile that

ripped into her heart, it was so strangely gentle and yet so at odds with the fiendish darkness of his eyes.

'Of course. I thought not.'

'If there is any explanation…'

For the sake of their past, the sake of the friend he had once been, she had to try just once more, though without any real hope.

'No. There is no explanation that I want to give you.'

It was a brutal, crushing dismissal, accompanied by a slashing gesture of one hand, cutting her off before she could complete the sentence.

'Nothing that would change a thing. So why don't we accept that as fact and move on?'

'Do we have anywhere to move on to?'

Where could they go from here? He had declared that everything she had heard about him was the truth. He had taken the weak, idealistic image she had once had of him and dashed it viciously to the ground, letting it splinter into tiny, irreparable shards that would never again let her form the picture of a wild but generous-spirited boy who had once been her rock, someone she could turn to when things got too bad to bear.

'I know my father's no saint, but you—you're hateful.'

She was past thinking now, past caring about what she said. Deep inside, where she prayed he would never be able to find it, she knew she was having to face up to the painful bitter truth. And that truth was that when she had found out the reality of what her father had been up to, what he had planned, then she had come running to find Alexei, to find her friend, hoping, believing that he of all people would be there for her, that he would help her. But the reality was that her friend Alexei no longer existed and this cold-eyed monster could be an even more deadly enemy than the cousin she feared so much.

'Not so hateful a moment ago,' Alexei tossed at her. 'Not when you were hungry for my kisses, my touch— for anything I would give you.'

'You took me by surprise!' Ria broke in sharply, knowing she was trying to avoid the image of herself he was showing her.

'And it was only the *surprise* that made you react as you did.'

'What else could there be?' Ria challenged, bringing up her chin as she glared her defiance at him, wanting to deny the cynicism that burned in his words. 'You're not so damn irresistible as you think…'

'Except when I have something that you want. So if I were to kiss you again…'

'No!'

It made her jump, taking a hasty step backwards, banging into the chair and almost sending it flying. The bruise stung sharply but nothing like the feeling inside as she faced the dark mockery in his face and knew that her reaction had only confirmed his worst suspicions.

'You wouldn't…' she tried again.

Her wary protest had his mouth curling at the corners, the sardonic humour more shocking than the cold anger of just moments before. She should have taken that anger as a warning, Ria acknowledged to herself. If anything, that should give her her cue to get out of here—fast. She had tried to persuade him to come back to Mecjoria. Tried to make him see that he was the best—the only—man who could take the throne. Tried and failed. And the worst realisation was the fact that she had miscalculated this so totally. She had thought that she was the best person for this task, but the truth was that she had really been the worst possible one. She had blundered in where she should have feared to tread, raising all the hatred and the anger he had been letting fester for ten long, bitter years and the only thing she could do was to walk out now while she could still hold her head high.

'Oh, but I would.' That dark mockery curled through his words like smoke around a newly extinguished candle, sending shivers of uncomfortable response sliding down her spine. 'And so would you, if you were prepared to be honest and admit it.'

'I wouldn't.'

She was shaking her head desperately even though she knew the vehemence of her response only betrayed her more, dug in deeper into the hole that was opening up around her feet. Impossibly she was actually wishing for the cold-eyed serpent back in place of that wicked smile, the calculated mockery.

'Liar.'

It was soft and deadly, terrifyingly so as he emphasised it with a couple of slow, deliberate steps towards her, and she could feel the colour coming and going in her cheeks as she tried to get a grip on the seesaw of emotions that swung sickeningly up and down inside her. It would be so much easier if her senses weren't on red alert in response to the potently masculine impact of his powerful form, the lean, lithe frame, the powerful chest and arms in contrast to the fine linen of his shirt. Her eyes were fixed on the bronzed skin of his throat and the dark curls of hair exposed by the open neckline. He was so close that she could see the faint shadow on his jaw where the dark growth of stubble was already beginning to appear, and the clean musky aroma of his skin, topped with the tang of some bergamot scent, was tantalising her nostrils.

The memory of that kiss was so sharp in her mind, the scent of his body bringing back to her how it had felt to be enclosed in his arms, feel the strength of muscle, the heat of his skin surrounding her. The trouble was that she did want him to kiss her—that was something she couldn't deny. It was there in the dryness of her mouth, the tightness of her throat so that she could barely breathe, let alone swallow. The heavy thuds of her heart against her ribs were a blend of excited anticipation and a shocking sense of dread. She wanted his kiss, wanted his touch— but she knew just what she would be unleashing if she allowed anything to happen. And she already had far too much to lose to take any extra risks.

'No lie,' she flung at him. 'Not then and not now. I can see I'm wasting my time here.'

'That's one thing we can agree on.'

It was when he swung away from her that she knew every last chance of being heard, or even getting him to give her a single moment's consideration, was over. The hard, straight line of his back was turned to her, taut and powerful as a stone wall against any appeal she might direct towards him. And the way his hands were pushed deep into the pockets of his trousers showed the fierce control he was imposing on himself and the volatile temper she sensed was almost slipping away from him.

'It seems that you're not going to be any use to me so I might as well call it a day.'

'Please do.'

If he stayed turned away, Alexei told himself, then he might just keep his wayward senses under control until she had left. It was shocking to find the way that cold fury warred with an aching burn of lust that held him in its grip, unable to move, unable to think straight.

In the moment that she had stood up and faced him he had known that the rush of hard, hot sensuality of a few moments before had not been a one-off. And that it was not something that was going to go away any time soon.

Something about the woman that Ria had become reached out and caught him in a net of sexual hunger, one that thudded heavily through his body, centring on the hardness between his legs. The fall of the shining darkness of her hair, the gleam of her beautiful almond-shaped eyes, the rose-tinted curve of her lips, shockingly touched with a sexual gleam of moisture where she had slicked her small pink tongue along them, had all woven a sensual spell around him, one he was struggling to free himself from. He could still taste her if he let his tongue touch his own lips, the scent of her skin was on his clothes, topped by that slight spicy floral scent she wore that made him want to press his lips; to her soft flesh, inhale the essence of her as he kissed her all over.

He still did. He still wanted to reach out and haul her into his arms, kiss her, touch her. She was the last person in the world he should feel this way about, the worst person in the world to have any sort of association with, let alone the hot passionate sex his body hungered for. She came with far too much baggage, not the least of which was the connection with Mecjoria, the country that had once been so much a part of his past and had almost destroyed him as a result. Everything about her threatened to drag him back into that past, to enclose him in the memories he hated, imprison him again in all that he had escaped from. Ria might tempt him—hell, the temptation she offered was so strong that he could feel it twining round him, tightening, like great coils of rope, almost impossible to resist—but he was not going to give in to it. It would only drag him back into the past he had barely walked away from, reduce him all over again to the boy he had once been, lonely, needy, and that was not going to happen.

And then she had done it again. She had turned that

look on him. The Grand Duchess Honoria look. It had hit him hard. It was the same look that she'd turned on him ten years before. He didn't know which was the worst, the fact that she still thought she could look at him in that way or the fact that it could still get to him. That she could still make him feel that way. As if all he had done and achieved had never been. As if he was still the Alexei who had hungered for approval and friendship, especially from her. From Ria. His friend.

No longer a friend. That was too innocent a word, and what he felt now was definitely not innocent. Hearing her voice and the way that something—pride? Anger? Defiance?—had hardened it, he knew what he was going to do, even if the roar of heat in his blood made it a struggle to make his body behave as his mind told him he should. Hungry sensuality and coldly rational thought fought an ugly little battle that tightened every muscle, twisted every nerve.

But it was a battle he was determined to win.

'I would appreciate it if you left now.'

It was something of a shock to find that echoes of the training his father had given him before the cancer had stolen even his voice had surfaced from his past to make him impose the sort of control over his tone that turned the formal politeness into an icy-cold distance. She would have had something of the same training so he didn't doubt that she knew exactly what that tone meant.

'But I can't...'

'But you can. You can accept that this is never going to happen—that you have failed. Whoever advised you to come here you should let them know that they sent quite the wrong person to plead their case. They would have done better to send your father—I might actually have listened to him more than I would to you.'

He heard her sharply indrawn breath and almost turned to see the reaction stamped on her face.

Almost. But he caught himself in time. He was not going to subject himself to that sort of temptation ever again.

'So now just go. I have nothing more to say to you, and I never want to see you in my life again.'

Would she fight him on this? Would she try once more to persuade him? Dear God, was he almost tempted by the thought that she might? Fiercely he fixed his gaze on the darkness beyond the window. A darkness in which he could see the faint reflection of her shape, the pale gleam of her skin, the dark pools of her eyes. The silence that followed his words was total, and it dragged on and on, it seemed, stretching over the space of too many heartbeats.

But then at last he saw her head drop slightly, acknowledging defeat. She turned one last look on him, but clearly thought better of even trying to speak as she twisted on her heel and headed for the door, slender back straight, auburn head held high.

It was only as the door swung to behind her, the wood thudding into the frame, that he realised how unconsciously he had used exactly the words that she had thrown at him in their last meeting in Mecjoria ten years before. She had been the one to turn and walk away then too, marching away from him without a backward glance, taking with her the last hope he had had.

Recalling how it had felt then, it was impossible not to remember all he had ever wanted and now could never have—all over again. He had wanted to belong, damn it, he'd tried. He'd thought that when his parents had reconciled that at last he'd found the father, the family, he'd always wanted. But his father's illness had meant that he had never had the time to make a reality out of that dream. It had all crumbled around him.

But this time it had been his own decision to throw it all away. He had had his revenge for the way she and her family had treated him, turning the tables on her completely and reversing the roles they had once had. It should have been what he wanted. It should have provided him with the sort of dark satisfaction that would have made these last ten years of exile and of struggle finally worthwhile. But the troubling thing was the uncomfortable sensation in the pit of his stomach that told him that satisfaction was the furthest thing from what he was feeling. If anything, he felt emptier and hungrier than ever before.

The royal document still lay on his desk where he had dropped it, and for a moment he let himself touch it, resting his fingers on the ornate signature next to the dark-red seal. The signature of his grandfather. King of Mecjoria.

King.

Just four letters of a word but it seemed to explode inside his head. Ria had offered him the chance to return to Mecjoria, not just as himself—but as its king.

It was ironic that Ria claimed to have come here today to ask him to take the crown—to be King of Mecjoria when all that her appearance had done was to bring home to him how totally unsuited he was for any such role. He had failed as a prince, but that had been as nothing when compared to his failure as a father. But she thought that she could persuade him that he was needed in her homeland.

Her homeland. Not his.

But then she had said that the only alternative was for Ivan to be king. What a choice. Poor Mecjoria. To be torn between a bully boy and a man who knew nothing at all about being a royal—let alone running a country. His father's country.

His father must be spinning in his grave at just the thought.

And yet his father had had Ivan sussed even all those years ago. From the corners of his memory came the recollection of a conversation—one of the very rare conversations—he had had with his dying father. Weak, barely able to open his eyes, let alone move, his father had known of the stand-up argument, almost a fight, Alexei had had with Ivan the previous day.

'That boy is trouble,' he had whispered. 'He's dangerous. Watch him—and watch your back when you're with him. Never let him win.'

And this was the man who could take over the throne— unless he stopped him.

Moving to the window, he looked down into the street to see Ria's tall, slim figure emerge from the front of the Sarova building and start to walk away down the street, pausing to cross at the traffic lights. He had wanted her to leave, so why did he now feel as if she was taking with her some essential part of him, something that made him whole?

The part he had once thought that Belle would fill.

'Hell, no.'

He turned away fiercely as the scene before him blurred disturbingly.

Did he really think that Ria would fill that hole in his life? It was just sex. Nothing but the reawakening of his senses that had started from the moment he had walked into the room and set eyes on her. And he had the disturbing feeling that there was only one way to erase the yearning sensations that tormented his body.

The only real satisfaction he could find would be to

have Ria—the Grand Duchess Honoria—in his bed so that he could sate himself in her body and so hope, at last, to erase the bitterness of memories that had been festering for far too long. But he had just destroyed his chances of ever having that happen. He had driven her away, and in that moment he had believed that that was the wisest, the only rational course.

Except of course that rationality had nothing to do with the burning sensuality of his reaction to her, the carnal storm that still pounded through him, even after she had left the room.

Rationality might tell him that walking away from her was the sanest path to take but the bruise of sexual hunger that made his body ache still left no room for sanity or rational thought. This restless, nagging feeling was so much like the way he had felt when he had first come to England, into exile with his mother, a feeling that he had thought he had subdued, even erased completely. One brief meeting with Ria had revived everything he had never wanted to feel ever again, but in the past those feelings had been those of a youth who had not long left boyhood behind. Now he was a grown man, with an experience of life, and Ria was a full-grown woman. He *wanted* Ria as he had never wanted another woman in his life, craved her like a yearning addict needing a fix, and he knew that these feelings would take far more than ten years longer to bury all over again—if, in fact, they could ever be truly buried at all.

He had vowed to himself that he would throw her out of his life and forget about her. Already he was regretting and rethinking that vow, knowing that forgetting her was going to be impossible. He was going to have her—but it had to be on his own terms.

CHAPTER SIX

'YOU MUST HAVE this wrong.'

Coming to a dead halt, Ria stood in the doorway, staring out across the airport tarmac, shaking her head in disbelief. The sleek, elegant jet that stood gleaming in the sunshine was not at all what she had been anticipating and she couldn't imagine why anyone should think that it was there for her.

When she had arrived at the airport for her flight home, she had been feeling more raw and vulnerable than she had ever been in her life. With her one hope gone, the future now stretched ahead of her and her country, dark and oppressive, with no way of rescue or escape unless she took the way her father had planned.

She certainly hadn't expected to be greeted by a man in uniform, swept through the briefest of security checks and delivered out here where the luxurious private jets of the rich, famous and powerful waited for permission to take off to whatever private island or sophisticated resort might be their ultimate destination.

'There really has to be some mistake...' she tried again, coming to an abrupt halt at the foot of the steps up to the plane, as he stood back to let her precede him.

'No mistake.'

The words came from above her, at the top of the steps,

and in spite of the noise of the wind blowing across the tarmac she knew immediately who had spoken.

The open door at the head of the steps was now filled with the tall, powerful figure of Alexei Sarova, the man she had believed she had left behind in London and would never, ever see again. Casually dressed in a loose white shirt and worn denim jeans, his hair blown about in the breeze, his powerful frame still had a heart-stopping impact, an effect that was multiplied a hundred times by his dominant position so high up above her.

'No mistake at all,' he said now, dark eyes locking with hers. 'I asked for you to be brought here.'

'You did? But why?'

'It seemed ridiculous to let you fly cattle class when we are both going to the same place.'

'We are?'

Had she heard right? Was he actually saying that he was flying to Mecjoria? Could he be thinking of agreeing to her request that he claim the throne? The man who had turned his back on her both physically and emotionally.

'We are. So are you going to stand there dithering for much longer or are you going to come up here and take your seat? Everything is ready for take-off but if we don't leave soon we will miss our allocated slot.'

'I'm not going anywhere with you.'

He couldn't have reversed that brutally unyielding decision in the space of less than twenty-four hours, could he? And yet if not then why was he here?

The slightest of adjustments in the way that he stood gave away the hint of a change in his mood—for the worse.

'So it really isn't a matter of life or death that I go to Mecjoria and look into the situation for the accession after all?'

As he echoed the description she'd given him, he managed to put a sardonic note on the words that twisted a knife even more disturbingly in her nerves. She didn't know why this was happening, she only knew that suddenly, for some reason, he seemed prepared to toss her a lifeline, one that she would be the greatest fool in the world to ignore.

'All right!'

Not giving herself any more time to think, Ria pushed herself into action, flinging one foot on to the steps and then the other, grabbing at the rail for support, almost tumbling to the ground at Alexei's feet as she reached the top.

What else could she do? She had spent last night wide awake and restless, going over the scene in his house again and again, berating herself for failing so badly, for driving him further away rather than persuading him round to her side. She had cursed herself for bringing her father into the discussion, seeing the black rage and hatred simply thinking of him had brought into his eyes. She had even reached for her phone a couple of times, wondering if she rang him that he might actually listen, and each time she had dropped it back down again, knowing that the man who had turned his back on her and told her to leave so brutally had no room in his mind or his heart for second thoughts or second chances. Today she'd faced the prospect of going back home knowing that everything was lost, and with no idea how she was going to face the future.

And then suddenly this...

'I don't understand.'

She was gasping as if she'd run a mile rather than just up a short flight of steps, but it was tension and not lack of fitness that caught her round her throat, making it impossible to breathe.

But Alexei was clearly in no mood to offer any explanations. Instead with a bruising grip on her arm he steered her out of the sunlight and into the plane where she blinked hard as her eyes adjusted to the change in light.

Once she would have been the one with access to a private plane. Not for her sole use, or even that of her family, but she had sometimes travelled with a member of the royal family, or accompanying her father in his official role. But it had never been like this. The Mecjorian royal plane had been as old-fashioned and stiffly formal as the regime itself, reflecting the views of the old king. This one was a symphony of cool calm, with pale bronze carpets, wide, soft seats just waiting for someone to sink into their creamy leather cushions. Everything was light and space, and spoke of luxury beyond price; and the impact of it hit like a blow, making her head spin.

Once again that unanswerable question pounded at her thoughts. Just why—*why*—would Alexei want Mecjoria, a small, insignificant, run-down Eastern European country, when he had all this? Why would he even spare a thought for the place or the chaos that would swamp the inhabitants if he refused the throne and let it pass to Ivan?

With his hand still on her arm, the heat of his palm burning through the soft pink cotton of her top and into her skin, the power and strength of his body so close beside her was overwhelming and almost shocking. In spite of the fact that he was so casually dressed, he carried himself with the sort of power that few men could show, making her heart kick hard against her ribs in a lethal combination of physical response and apprehension.

'Take a seat.'

Ria was grateful to sink down into the enveloping comfort of the nearest seat, her legs disturbingly unsteady beneath her. The air seemed suddenly too thick to breathe, the roar of the engines as the pilot prepared the plane for flight too loud in her ears so that she couldn't think straight or do anything other than obey him. She was on her way to Mecjoria and, for his own private reasons, Alexei was with her. That and the powerful thrust of the plane as it set off down the runway was more than enough to cope with at the moment.

'Fasten your seatbelt.'

Alexei was clearly not going to take the trouble to enlighten her on anything—not yet anyway, as he took the seat opposite her, long legs stretched out, crossed at the ankles—and settled himself, ready for take-off.

She was dismissed from his thoughts as he turned his head, focussing his attention through the window to where the green of the grass on the side of the runway was now flashing past at an incredible speed as the plane raced towards take-off. Another couple of minutes and the wheels had left the ground, the jet soaring away from the ground and up into the sky. The impact pushed Ria back into her seat, her head against the rest, her hands clutching the arms of her chair. Unexpectedly, unbelievably, she had another chance and she was going to take it if she possibly could.

But that added a whole new burden of worry to the nervousness she was already feeling. Just for a moment her thoughts reeled. Had she done the right thing coming here? Was she justified in putting her own family, her own personal needs, first like this? It was true that she feared the consequences if Ivan took the crown. She dreaded the thought of what it meant for her personally if she had to follow her father's plans for that event, but how did she know if Alexei would be any better? The memory of the stories of his life in London that had been reported in the papers back home came back to haunt her. There had been one where he had been caught unaware, his hand half-lifted to his face to escape the flash of the camera. But he hadn't been quick enough to conceal the fact that he had obviously been in a fight; that his eye was blackened, his nose bloodied.

And of course there had been his neglect of his poor little daughter. A neglect that he hadn't even tried to deny. Was she right in bringing such a man back to Mecjoria— as its king?

But he was the rightful king. That was the one argument she was totally sure of.

The plane had reached its cruising height and had straightened out of the steep climb but Ria's stomach was still knotted in that unnerving tension that the fast ascent, combined with her own inner turmoil, had created. She had a dreadful feeling of no going back, knowing that she could only go forward—though she had no idea where that might lead.

'Would you like a drink? Something to eat?'

It was perfectly polite, the calm enquiry of a courteous host as a slightly raised hand summoned an attendant who jumped to attention as if she had just been waiting for the signal.

'Some coffee would be nice.' She hadn't been able to eat any breakfast before she left for the airport. 'We do have almost five hours to fill.'

'I don't think you need to worry about filling time on this flight,' Alexei told her. 'We'll have plenty to keep us occupied.'

'We will?' It was sharp and tight with a new rush of nerves.

In contrast, Alexei looked supremely relaxed, lounging back in his seat opposite her as he nodded.

'You have…' he checked the workmanlike heavy watch on his wrist '…four hours to convince me that I should even consider taking up the crown of Mecjoria and allowing myself to be declared king.'

'But I thought—I mean—you're here now. And we're heading for…'

The words shrivelled on her tongue as she looked into the cold darkness of his face and saw that there was nothing there to give her confidence that this was all going to work out right.

'I'm here now,' he agreed soberly, dark eyes hooded and shadowed. 'And we are on a flight path for Mecjoria—for the capital. This plane will land there, if only to let you off so you can go and talk to the courtiers who sent you. But that does not mean that I will disembark as well.'

His tone was flat, emotionless, unyielding, and looking into his eyes was like staring into the icy depth of a deep, deep lake, frozen over with a coating of thick black ice, bleak and impenetrable. He had made one tiny concession and that was all he was going to let her have—unless she could convince him otherwise.

'Our estimated time of arrival is five in the afternoon, Mecjorian time. You have until then to persuade me that I should not just turn round and head home as soon as we have let you disembark.'

He meant it, she had no doubt about that, and a sensation like cold slimy footsteps crept down her back. The thought of being so near yet so far curdled in her stomach. The attendant appeared with her coffee and she took refuge in huddling over the cup as if the warmth from the hot liquid might melt the ice that seemed to have frozen right through to her bones. Just when she had thought she could relax, that Alexei was heading for Mecjoria, and taking her with him to return home—if not in triumph then at least with some hope of success and a more positive future for the country—suddenly he had shown that he had been working on a totally different plan.

It didn't help at all that she was sitting opposite the most devastatingly attractive man she had ever seen in her whole life. Her schoolgirl crush on the adolescent Alexei seemed like froth and bubble compared to the raw, gut-deep sensual impact of his adult self on all that was female inside her. If he so much as moved, her senses sprang to life, heat and moisture pooling between her thighs so that she shifted uncomfortably in her seat, crossing and uncrossing her legs restlessly.

'I told you...'

Another smile was a swift flash on and off, one that put no light in his eyes.

'Tell me again.' It was a command, not a suggestion. 'We have plenty of time.'

It was going to be interesting to see if she came up with exactly the same arguments as she had given him yesterday, Alexei reflected. Arguments that would change his way of life; hell, his whole future if the decision he had come to in the middle of the night was anything to go by. He hadn't been able to sleep and had spent long hours surfing the Internet, researching the situation in Mecjoria even more intensely than usual, finding out as much as he possibly could. There was plenty he already knew. In spite of the mask of indifference he had hidden behind when Ria had confronted him, he had kept a careful eye on all that was happening in his father's homeland ever since he and his mother had been exiled from the place. His research had told him that everything she had said was true, but this time, driven to dig more deeply, he had found there was more to it than that. That there was one vital element to this whole succession business that he had never suspected, and that she had not revealed.

And that was something that changed everything.

Why had she not told him the full truth? What did she have to gain from keeping it from him?

In the seat opposite, Ria stirred slightly, the soft sound of her denim-clad legs sliding across each other setting his senses on red alert in a heartbeat. It was hell to sit here with his body hardening in response to just the thought of her being there, so close and yet so far away. He should never have touched her, never have let the feel of the warm velvet of her skin, the scent of her hair, start off the heavy pulse of hunger that was like a thickness in his blood. It stopped him thinking straight and made him *want*. And wanting was going to have to be put aside for now, for a time at least. He had her just where he wanted her, and he wasn't going to let her get away. But first he was going to make her acknowledge that this was the only way that it could be. The sensual pleasure he anticipated would be one thing. Bringing her to admit that she had nowhere else to go would add a whole new dimension of satisfaction to his revenge on the family that had been responsible for his and his mother's exile from the country where they belonged.

'Persuade me.'

With no other alternative, Ria had to go over it all again. The one thing she didn't do was to mention anything about personal involvement. Deep down inside she knew instinctively that that could only act against her. She knew now how much he hated her family, how he would do anything rather than help them in any way. It was perhaps an hour and a half later that she stopped, drawing in a much-needed breath, reaching for the glass of water that had replaced the coffee of earlier. Gulping down the drink she had left ignored as she focussed totally on the man opposite her, she struggled to ease the discomfort of her parched throat as she waited for his response.

It was a long time coming. A long, uncomfortable time as he subjected her to a burning scrutiny. Like her he reached for his crystal tumbler of iced water but the swallow he took was long, slow and indolently relaxed.

'Very interesting,' he drawled, leaning back in his seat, never taking his eyes off her for a moment. 'But you neglected to explain that the situation is not quite as simple as you made out. There's one more thing I want to know.'

'Anything.' She didn't care if she sounded close to desperate. That was how she felt, so why try to hide it at this delicate stage?

'Anything?' There was a definite challenge in the darkeyed look he slanted in her direction. 'Then tell me about the marriage.'

'The—the marriage…'

Ria's stomach twisted painfully, her discomfort made all the worse by the way that the plane had suddenly hit a patch of turbulence and lurched violently, dropping frighteningly, down and then back up again.

'Yes, the marriage your father has arranged for you. I am the heir to the throne if the individual positions in the hierarchy—the direct line—are considered. On my own, I have the stronger claim—if I want it.'

There it was again, that note of threat that he might refuse the crown, and leave her stranded without a hope of finding any other way out—as she now suspected he had known all along. How he must have enjoyed watching her perform all over again, knowing all the while that he understood the real truth of her position, the cleft stick she was caught in with little hope of escape.

'But you omitted to point out that it is not just Ivan who also has a distant potential claim to the throne.'

The glass he held was placed on the table with deliberate care. The same control showed as he stood up, big and dark and lean, towering over her and making even the space of the luxurious jet feel confined and restricted in a sudden and shocking way. Forced to raise her head to look up at him, she found that the air in the cabin seemed to have thickened and grown heavier.

'You forgot to say…' His tone made it plain that he didn't think for a moment she had forgotten anything. 'that you and Ivan have a unique connection where the crown is concerned. Individually his claim is so much weaker, but *together* you would be almost unassailable.'

Ria could almost feel the blood draining from her face. She must look like a ghost, and that would show him how perfectly he had hit the mark.

'There is no together!'

His gesture might have been flicking away a fly, it was so scornfully dismissive of her protest.

'Are you saying that none of this is true? That Ivan's claim to the throne is clear and open, with no other help needed—and you won't need him to free your father, restore your family fortunes to the way they used to be?'

He made it sound so mercenary. But then what had she expected from a man who so blatantly despised her and every member of her family?

'No—'

There was no togetherness between Ivan and her. Nothing except the one that had been forced on her, that she would have to accept if Alexei didn't listen to her pleas. The prospect of freedom from the future she dreaded that had seemed to open up before her now seemed to be moving further away with every breath she took. Ria pushed herself to her feet, needing the greater strength of a position facing him on a much better level, her green eyes meeting his head-on.

'I mean, yes, it's true that if I marry him his right to the throne is strengthened...'

'Isn't it *when* you marry him?' Alexei slipped in, cold and deadly. 'I understand that the contract has already been signed.'

By her father. Without any consultation or even her knowledge. She had been used as a pawn in the political bargaining.

'I— How did you find out that?' How could he know about the contract her father had made with Ivan, when she had only become aware of it herself just days before?

'I have my sources.'

He'd been up all night, and he'd called in all his contacts, investigating exactly what was behind this sudden desire of hers to have him as king in Mecjoria. All the time she had been talking yesterday—and again just now—he had sensed she was holding something back, keeping something hidden. He had never expected that it would be this.

Once he had found the real explanation he had been unable to think of anything else. Because this turned everything upside down from the way he'd seen everything at first. He'd been convinced that Ria had brought him the document that proved his parents' marriage valid, and that he was the rightful king, because that would give her— and her family—an advantage if he came to the throne. She was softening him up so that he would release her father, restore the family fortunes...

The discovery of the proposed marriage to Ivan Kolosky made a nonsense out of all that. Even more so because she had never said a word about it.

That marriage would give her everything she wanted—and more. It would make her Queen of Mecjoria and he knew that had always been Gregor Escalona's deepest ambition. The reason why he had insisted on his daughter's immaculate behaviour, training her to be the perfect young royal, controlling every move, every decision she made. It was the reason why Gregor had betrayed his father's memory by bringing the legitimacy of his marriage into question. So why had she even brought the marriage certificate to him in the first place? And why had she never mentioned the proposed marriage to Ivan?

Last night he had thought he had decided on a way to play this that would give him retribution for all that had happened to him and his mother when they had been exiled from their home, losing every last penny of the fortune that should have been theirs, his mother's good name along with it, but at last it seemed that payback was within his grasp.

But one more discovery and everything had changed. There was more on offer now. More than he could ever have dreamed of. He wanted more. And there was one way he was sure of getting it.

'So now how about you tell me the real truth?'

He saw the wariness in her eyes, the shadow that crossed her face, and it made him all the more determined to get to the bottom of all of this.

He'd planned on giving her another chance to give him the real facts this morning, but the truth was that as soon as she'd started to speak his concentration had been shot to pieces. All he could focus on was the way she looked, with that dark auburn hair pulled back into a pony tail so that it exposed the fine bone structure of her features, the brilliance of her eyes. Tiny silver earrings sparkled in her lobes, seeming to catch the flash of her eyes as she leaned towards him, elegant hands coming up to emphasise her points. The movement of her mouth fascinated him, the soft rose-tinted curve of her lips moving to emphasise what she had to say, the faint sheen of moisture on them making him want to lean forward and kiss her hard and fierce, plunge his tongue into her open mouth and taste her again as he had done the night before.

She hadn't said anything about Ivan and that made him grit his teeth tight against the questions that needed answers. Now he couldn't look at her without thinking about Ivan—and about her with Ivan. Acid rose in his throat at just the thought of it and the blood heated in his veins, making his heart punch harshly, a pulse throbbing near his temple. The thought of her with anyone else—anyone but him—was too much to take. But with *Ivan*...

And that feeling—that fury of jealousy, the hunger, that sensation of being alive that had been missing in his life for so long—told him so much. It erased the numbness he had been living—existing—with, the deadness that had invaded his world since the loss of first his father, and later the baby daughter he had barely started to get to know. He hadn't felt this way in years and he wanted it back. And he wanted Ria, as the woman who had given sensation back to him.

'That if you can't persuade me to take the throne, then you are tied into a contract to marry Ivan, and so strengthen his claim to the inheritance. Tell me—why not just go with the marriage to Ivan? After all it would make you Queen of Mecjoria.'

'My father might want that, perhaps, but not me!'

But this was what her father had been training her for, the summit of her family's ambitions. And if being queen had been her ambition too then all she had had to do was to leave the marriage document where it was.

'You don't want to be queen?'

'And you want to be king?' she tossed back, earning herself a faint, twisted smile and an ironical inclination of his head in acknowledgement of the hit. But she hadn't spent the past ten years exiled from the country he was now supposed to rule.

'Where was the marriage certificate found?' he demanded now, wanting to get at the truth.

It was a question she didn't want to answer, that much was obvious, and yet he didn't think she was trying to deceive him. Sharp white teeth dug into the softness of her lower lip, and he was suddenly assailed by the impulse to protest at the damage she was doing to the delicate skin. Instead he made himself repeat the question in order to divert his thoughts.

'Where?'

Her delicate chin came up defiantly, gold-green eyes blazing into his.

'My father had it all the time. It was in his safe when I checked in there after he was arrested. My mother begged me to look for something that might help.' Once more her teeth worried at her lip as she obviously had to push herself to go on. 'I also found the contract between him and Ivan then.'

'You hadn't known before?'

He could well believe that of Gregor, conspiring with anyone he could in secret. But would he really sign his daughter's life away without her knowing?

'I knew nothing about it!' There was the tremor of real horror in her voice.

'Your father can't force you into this.'

Her soft mouth twisted into an expression of resignation—or was it bitterness?

'In Mecjoria, royalty—even unimportant royalty like

me—don't expect to marry for love. Dynastic contracts matter so much more than personal feelings. And right now peace is what matters. I meant everything I said about the possible consequences if the succession isn't easy and smooth. If not you, then Ivan is the only logical candidate.'

'But neither of us wants Ivan to take the throne.'

'No, we both know what a disaster that would be.'

The way she rushed to agree with him, the tone in which she did it, scraped roughly across his exposed skin. The mood of calm and control that had come from feeling that he had her just where he wanted her was starting to fray at the edges, coming unravelled with every breath he drew in. Last night she had claimed she'd given him every argument she possessed but she'd kept this vital point carefully back. And hiding that point showed him just how much she had wanted to influence him into agreeing to her plans without ever knowing the full story.

She had only forced herself to come to him because she had no possible alternative. Because her country needed it now that she had proof that he wasn't illegitimate, that he was truly as royal as she was—more. But because she needed it too. Would she have told him about the document if she hadn't also been able to use it to her own advantage? Because she wasn't prepared to sacrifice her own freedom in order to rescue the place herself. She hadn't reckoned on him ever finding out about the proposed union between her family and Ivan's—at least not until it was too late.

'So you will do as I ask? You will take the throne?'

There was a very different mood in the words, with a whole new sparkle in those eyes, a lift to the warm curve of her mouth. She thought she had got what she wanted from him—that she had worked out a way of ensuring an heir to the throne but without her having to tie herself into marriage with the only other candidate for the crown. So that he could live the restricted, controlled life of a royal while she kept her freedom and could live as she pleased.

He felt used, manipulated. But it didn't stop him wanting her.

And wanting her didn't stop him recognising that her father had done a good job in training her up to be a queen—whoever's wife she might be. From acknowledging what an asset she would be as anyone's consort—and it didn't have to be Ivan's. He didn't want her to be Ivan's any more than she did.

'I could be persuaded,' he said slowly.

The light that her smile brought to her eyes almost made him lose his grip on his temper as icy rage swamped him. She thought she was winning and that pushed him dangerously close to the edge. All he wanted was to pull the rug out from under her, let her know that he already had all her secrets and he fully intended to use them to his own advantage.

But there was more pleasure in letting things out bit by bit than in dumping everything on her all at once.

'I will do as you ask,' he said slowly, keeping his eyes locked on her face to enjoy watching her reaction. 'But there are terms.'

CHAPTER SEVEN

'TERMS?' RIA ECHOED the word on a note of pure horror. 'What sort of terms?'

'Terms that you and I need to agree between us. We need to plan the future.'

'But we have no future…'

She looked so appalled at the thought of any more time spent with him. She would even refute the flames that burned between them if she could. It was there in the darkness that clouded her eyes, the way she was fighting to deny there was anything between them.

'You think?'

Their eyes clashed, held for a moment. Hers were the first to drop as she recognised the unyielding challenge in his.

'What terms?' she asked.

So much of the attack had gone out of her voice, leaving it weakened and deflated. Was it possible that she suspected what was coming? A dark wave of satisfaction flooded through his veins.

'I will be king—on the same conditions as it would have been for Ivan to take the throne.'

It took a moment for her to register just what he had said, several more to have the words sink in and the meaning behind the flat statement become real. He watched every change of emotion spill across her face, the way that it tightened the muscles around her mouth and jaw, made her elegant throat contract on a hard swallow. One that he felt echo in his own throat as he fought the urge to press his lips to the pale skin of her neck and follow the movement down.

'But those conditions were only for Ivan…' Ria stammered.

She still hadn't quite realised just what he was talking about. Either that or she didn't want to accept that he could actually mean it.

'It's that or nothing. And I wish you joy being Ivan's wife.'

'And the country?' She'd found some new strength from somewhere, enough to challenge him. 'Are you prepared for the civil unrest that will follow if you walk away now?'

That caught him up sharp. Took him back to the darkness of the night where his memories of his father's dying words had forced him to face the prospect of a future in which the repercussions of his decisions, his actions, reverberated out into the coming days and years with the possibility of guilt and the dreadful responsibility of the wrong choices made in anger. He'd been there once before and it was a hell he had no wish to return to. He'd let someone—not just anyone, he'd let *Belle*—down because of that anger once and even after years the stab of memory, of guilt, was brutal. Was he going to do it again? Let down a whole nation? Thousands of families—hundreds of Belles?

He'd be letting down his father too if he let Ivan take over the throne, ignoring the warning Mikail had given him.

If he stayed angry, that was always the risk. But this,

this was a decision he had made in cold blood. To defeat Ivan. And her father. And to have Ria at his side as his queen and in his bed.

'There is one way to ensure that doesn't happen. And to keep Ivan from the crown at the same time. Believe me, I feel the same as you do at the thought of him ruling Mecjoria.'

She should have expected this, Ria told herself. She knew how much he and Ivan had loathed each other back in the days when they had all lived at the court when the old king had been alive. She should have remembered how the other man had sneered at everything Alexei did, and had made appallingly insulting remarks about his mother—the commoner who had dared to think that she could become a member of the royal family.

A few moments before she had been afraid of the direction in which his thoughts seemed to be heading, but this… Was it possible that he meant that they could work together on this? The thought of doing something with Alexei rather than fighting him for everything made her heart twist on a little judder of excitement. She had hoped to have her friend Alexei back in her life. She had never dreamed it might actually happen.

But did her friend Alexei still exist? Did she want him to? That friend had never made her feel this way. This very adult, very female, very sexual way.

'Exactly what terms are you talking about?' Deep down, she feared she knew but she couldn't believe it.

'I told you. I will accept the throne on the same conditions as would have applied if Ivan was to inherit. The ones your father agreed—and it seems you were prepared to go along with.'

Ria's head went back, her eyes widening. The ice-blooded statement slammed into her mind with the force of a lightning bolt, making her head spin sickeningly. It was like reliving the moment she had found the signed agreement amongst her father's papers, but somehow worse. She had always known her father was an arch manipulator—but Alexei? She'd gone to him with such hope, but now it seemed that she was trapped even more than before. And her own impulsive declaration of just moments before had just entangled her further in this dark spider's web.

'Marriage.' It was dull and flat, the death knell to the hopes she had only just allowed to creep into her mind. 'The terms of that agreement were marriage.'

He didn't respond; didn't even incline his head in any indication of agreement. Just blinked hard, once, and then those black, black eyes were fixed on her face, as unmoving and unyielding as the rest of him.

'You want me to *marry* you?' The words tasted like poison on her tongue. 'Just like that? I won't—I can't!'

'Not what you'd hoped for?' he enquired sardonically, the corners of his mouth curling into a cynical trace of a smile. 'The prospect doesn't appeal as much as being married to Ivan?'

'It doesn't appeal at all.'

The truth was that it was far worse.

She had never had any feeling except of fear and dislike for Ivan. Hadn't once loved him. Had never dreamed of the prospect of a future with him. Hadn't let herself imagine the possibility of loving and being loved by him as she had once dreamed of happening with Alexei.

So now to be proposed to... No, not proposed to—*propositioned*—so coldly, so heartlessly by him tore at her heart until she thought it must be bleeding to death inside.

She didn't want to look at him, couldn't bear to look into his face, and yet she found that she could look nowhere else. Those deep, dark eyes seemed to draw her in; the sculpted beauty of his mouth was a sensual temptation that she fought to resist. Once she'd dreamed of being kissed by those lips. Lying awake in her adolescent bed, she had imagined how it would feel, longed for it to be reality. Last night that dream had come true. She knew now how that mouth kissed, knew how it tasted, and the reality had been as sensually wonderful as she had hoped. It had left her with a hunger to feel those sensual lips on all the other, more intimate parts of her body. But all the time it had been tainted with a poison that threatened to destroy her emotionally.

And once she had dreamed of a marriage proposal from those lips too. But not like this.

'You can't really believe this is possible.'

'Why not? You've already admitted that neither of us wants Ivan on the throne—but if we made a pact to work together we could ensure that never happens, ensure peace for Mecjoria. You say I am the rightful king—you would make a good queen. After all, that was what your father trained you for.'

'I brought you that document because you are the rightful king!'

'And because you didn't want to marry Ivan.'

How could she deny that when it was nothing but the truth?

'My father had delusions of grandeur.' She tried to focus on his face but his powerful features blurred before her eyes. 'That's not the same as tying myself to someone I barely know.'

'You would have agreed to just this with Ivan.' Alexei pushed the point home. 'You said yourself that the royal family doesn't expect to marry for love.'

No, but they could dream of it—and she had dreamed…
Dreams that were now crashing in pieces around her.

'You'd simply be exchanging one political marriage
for another. What if I promise your father's freedom too?'

'You'd do that?' It was something she'd thought she'd
have to give up on, no matter how much her mother had
begged her to plead for Gregor's release.

'For you as my queen—yes, I'd do it. Oh, I don't expect a wedding right here and now—or even one as soon
as we land. I have the proclamation—the accession—to
deal with first.'

He actually sounded as if he thought that he was making some huge concession. The truth was that in his mind,
he *was* making that concession, obviously. He would give
her a breathing space—a short, barely tolerable breathing
space. But the ruthless, cold determination stamped on his
face told her that was all she would get. And it would be
only the barest minimum of time that he would allow her.

'Well, that's a relief!' Shock and horror made her voice
rigid and cold as she fought against showing the real depth
of her feelings. Her shoulders were so tight that they hurt
and her mouth ached with the control she was imposing
on it. 'Do you expect me to thank you?'

'No more than you should expect me to thank you for
cooperating in this.'

'I haven't said yet that I will cooperate!'

'But you will.' It was coldly, cruelly confident. No
room for argument or doubt. 'And you have to admit that
we have far more between us than you would ever have
had with Ivan.'

'I— No!'

She didn't know how she had managed to sit still so
long. She only knew that she couldn't do it now. She
pushed herself to her feet, up and away from him. From

his oppressive closeness, the dangerous warmth of his hard, lean frame, the disturbing scent of his skin that tantalised her senses. She wanted to go further—so much further—but in the cabin there wasn't enough space to run and hide. And at the same time her need to get away warred with a sensual compulsion to turn back into his atmosphere, to throw herself close against him and recapture that wild enticement that had swamped her totally on the previous night.

'Sit down!'

It was pure command, harsh and autocratic, flung at her so hard that she almost felt the words hit her in the back.

It took all her control to turn and face him, bringing her chin up in defiance so as not to let him see the turmoil she was feeling.

'What's this then, Alexei? Practising for when you're king?'

His scowl was dark and dangerous, making her shift uncomfortably where she stood, the movement aggravated by the lurch of the aircraft so that she almost lost her footing. Stubbornly she refused to reach out and grab the back of the nearest seat for support, however much she needed it.

'According to you, I will need all the practice I can get,' he shot back, the ice in his tone taking the temperature in the cabin down ten degrees or more. 'A commoner jumped up from the gutter, with no true nobility to speak of.'

'That was Ivan, not me!' Ria protested.

'Ivan—your prospective husband.'

She knew he was watching for her instinctive shudder but all the same she couldn't hold it back in spite of knowing how much she was giving away.

'But there is some truth in there—so there's another

reason why this marriage will work out,' Alexei continued coldly. 'I can give you the status and the fortune you want…'

Ria opened her mouth in a rush, needing to tell him that she didn't want either. But a swift, brutal glare stopped her mid-breath.

'And you—well you can be the civilising influence I need. You can teach me how to handle the court procedures—the etiquette I'll need to function as king.'

He almost sounded as if he meant it. Was it possible? Could he really be feeling a touch of insecurity here—and being prepared to admit to it? There was no way it seemed possible. But that twist to his mouth tugged on something deep inside her.

'But you grew up at court—for some years at least. You must have learned…'

'The basics, perhaps. But most of it I have forgotten. I didn't exactly see any use for it in the life I'm living now. And, as your father was so determined to point out, I was never really civilised.' The bite of acid in the words seemed to sear into Ria's skin, making her rub her hands down her arms to ease the burning sensation. 'Not quite blue-blooded enough.'

'Well, I'm sure you'll remember it quickly—without any help from me.'

'Ah, but I'm sure I'll pick it up faster with you at my side—as my partner and consort. My wife.'

'I won't do it.' She shook her head violently, sending her hair flying around her face.

Another lurch of the plane, more violent this time, made her stumble. She almost expected to hear the sound of shattering dreams falling to the floor as the movement coincided with the loss of all those hopes she had once had for the word 'wife' coming from this man.

'You can't make me.'

'I won't have to. You've done it to yourself already.'

As Ria watched in stunned disbelief, Alexei seemed to change mood completely, subsiding into his seat again and relaxing back against the soft, buttery leather.

'Let's see now—where shall I begin? Ah yes—the er-uminium mines.'

She knew then what was coming, acknowledging an aching sense of despair as she watched him lift one long-fingered hand and tick off his points across it one by one. All the arguments she had ever brought to bear on the subject of his possible accession to the throne, all the reasons she had given why he had to take the crown, to prevent Ivan doing so, to protect the country and to avoid civil unrest. They were now all repeated but turned upside down, twisted back against her, landing sharp as poisoned darts in her bruised soul. Alexei used them to provide evidence of the fact that she had no choice. That she had to do as he demanded or prove herself a liar and a traitor to everything she had held dear.

And break her mother's heart and health—possibly her mind too—if she left her father mouldering in his prison cell, as she had feared she was going to do when she had failed to bring Alexei back with her.

She had no choice. Or, rather, she did have a choice but it was between being trapped into this marriage and honouring the contract her father had made with Ivan. An arranged marriage to a man she loathed and feared. A man who made her skin crawl. Or a cold-blooded union to Alexei who would give her a marriage without love. A marriage with no heart. A marriage of shattered dreams.

'Do I have to go on?' Alexei enquired.

'Don't trouble yourself.' She dripped the sarcasm so

strongly that she fully expected it to form a pool at her feet. 'I think I can guess the rest.'

She couldn't see any way out of it. He had tied her up with her own arguments, left her without a leg to stand on. Looking at him now—at the ice that glazed his eyes, the cold, hard set of his face—the momentary hesitation, if that was what she had seen earlier, now seemed positively laughable. She had to have been imagining things.

'Good, so now we understand each other. I said *sit down,* Ria.' One lean hand pointed to the seat she had vacated.

Fury spiked, making her see sparks before her eyes.

'Don't order me around, Alexei! You don't have the right.'

'Oh, but I do,' he inserted smoothly. 'That is, I do if I am to do as you want. As king I can command and you…'

'You're not king yet.'

'Perhaps not, but we are approaching Mecjoria.' A nod towards the window indicated the way that the deep blue of the sea over which they had been flying had now given way to a wild coastline, a range of mountains. 'Any moment now we will be coming in to land. You should sit down and fasten your seatbelt.'

Was that the quirk of a smile at the corners of his mouth? Knowing she was beaten, Ria forced herself forward, dumping down into the seat with her teeth digging hard into her tongue to hold back the wave of anger that almost escaped her. Focussing her attention on snapping on her seatbelt, she addressed the man opposite with her head still bent.

'I had it wrong earlier, Alexei. You don't need any practice, you have the autocratic tyrant down pat—absolutely perfect. No need for anyone at your side to support you or to instruct you in any of the etiquette needed.'

'Perhaps so.'

His tone was infuriatingly relaxed, disturbingly assured.

'But you know as well as I do that the one way to settle this accession situation once and for all and to bring peace to the country for the future is to have someone with an unassailable right on the throne. Mecjoria rejected me once—what's to stop them doing it again? But you as queen will bring that unassailable right along with you. You can choose to give it to me—or to Ivan.'

Choose. There was the word that hit home, sticking in her throat like a piece of broken glass.

She didn't *have* a choice. She had set out on this mission to make sure that Ivan didn't become king—and that she didn't have to marry him. She'd achieved one aim but only by painting herself into a corner to do it. Alexei would be king, if she married him. She could escape the loveless arranged marriage to Ivan only if she agreed to a different one with Alexei.

Out of the frying pan and into the fire.

The way that the plane swayed and jumped, turning into a new course, and the change in the sound of its engines brought home to her the fact that they were circling, ready to approach the airport and the runway on which the jet would land very soon.

This plane will land there, if only to let you off... Alexei's words came back to haunt her. *But that does not mean that I will disembark as well.*

Marriage to Ivan or marriage to Alexei? She knew which one was better for the country—but right now she was thinking on a very personal level and that made everything so very different. The thought of both marriages made her shudder inside, but with very different responses.

One was a sense of cold horror of being tied to a bully like Ivan. For the other, the instinctive fear she was a prey to blended with a shiver of dangerous, treacherous excitement. The memory of last night and the rush of raw, carnal response that had flooded through her when Alexei had taken her in his arms, when he had kissed her, made it impossible to think beyond how it might feel to know that again.

The marriage would be a pretence but that would be real. She wouldn't be able to hide the hunger she felt or even attempt to disguise it.

'You call that a choice? You know I can't let Ivan take the crown. The results for the country would be so appalling.'

'And how do you know that I will not be as bad?'

She could only stare at him, asking herself the same question and finding no answer for it. She knew about Ivan's alliances with dangerous governments, his profligate habits, his cold nature, but the reality was that she knew nothing about Alexei other than the reports in the papers she had read. But she did know that like her he wanted to make sure Ivan didn't inherit.

'For me or for the country?'

'I thought we had agreed that we were largely irrelevant in this. It is the future of Mecjoria and her people that matters. It isn't personal.'

But he had made it personal with this cold-blooded proposition.

'It certainly isn't personal. It's dynastic necessity, pure and simple.

'You don't need to look as if you're facing imminent execution, Ria,' Alexei continued dryly. 'I'm not a monster. I don't expect you to take your marriage vows as soon as we land. For now all that I ask of you is that you

take your place as my promised bride. My devoted fiancée,' he added pointedly. 'No one must doubt that this is
a real relationship. A whirlwind romance perhaps, but
very definitely real.'

Could the atmosphere in the luxurious cabin get any
colder? Ria asked herself as she swallowed down his statement. Could there be any less emotion in his tone?

A sudden violent jolt, the screech of brakes, the rumble
of tyres on the runway brought her to the realisation that
they were down, had landed and the plane was now taxi-
ing towards the airport building. They had arrived; they
were on Mecjorian soil.

Peering out of the window, she saw the sun-baked
countryside that was familiar, the range of mountains
over in the distance, their tops covered in a coating of
snow. It should have felt like coming home. It was home.
She had only been away for less than a week, one hundred and twenty hours at the most, but it seemed that everything had changed totally. Her life was no longer her
own; her future had taken a totally different path from
the one she had believed it would follow. She had thought
that she would persuade Alexei to take the throne and then
she could quietly retreat into the background, live her life
in private. Now it seemed that instead she was going to
have to be up front and centre.

With Alexei.

Awkwardly she fumbled with her seatbelt, feeling imprisoned, tied down and needing desperately to be free.
But the way her future was going it seemed she would
never be free. She had gone to Alexei in the hope of being
freed from the future that her father had planned for her
but instead she had come up against a man who was even
more ruthless and controlling than Gregor had ever been.

As a result she had jumped out of the frying pan and right into the fire. And she faced the prospect of being burned alive as a result.

CHAPTER EIGHT

'Let me...'

Alexei had already dispensed with his seatbelt with clinical efficiency and he was standing beside her, his hand reaching out for the awkward buckle on hers. When he bent his head to deal with it the softness of his dark hair brushed against her cheek, caressing her skin and sending shivers of response down her spine. She could smell the citrus shampoo on his hair, the clean scent of his skin, and up this close she could see how already, even at this stage of the day, the dark shadow of the growth of beard marked his cheeks.

Her heart thudded in her throat and she had to sit back and clench her hands into tight fists down at her sides to stop herself from giving in to the urge to reach out and stroke his cheek, feel the contrast between warm satin skin and the rough scrape of hair against her fingertips. Heat flooded every part of her, pooling at the spot just between her legs, so close to where those strong, square-tipped fingers had just completed their task.

Would this instant, shockingly primitive reaction to his nearness make the future he had dictated to her so much easier or so very much harder? She didn't know and with sparks of response flaring in her brain, spots rising in front of her eyes, she couldn't even begin to think

of finding a way to answer her own question. She didn't
even know if she could get to her feet, the muscles in her
legs, even her bones, seeming to have melted in the burn
of response that possessed her.

'I can't…' she began but then, afraid of what she might
be revealing, swallowed down the admission and changed
it to, 'I don't think I can do this. How does a devoted fiancée—your devoted fiancée—behave?'

'You need to ask that? Here…'

Those strong hands came down again, clamping over
hers as he straightened up. He hauled her upwards, lifting her to her feet, so fast so roughly that she fell against
him, her breasts thrust into the hard, muscled planes of
his chest, her face pressed to the lean column of his throat,
her senses swimming from immediate sensual overload.

'Of course I need to ask!' Her physical response thickened her tone, making it husky and raw, alien in her own
ears. 'I'm not your fiancée—nor am I devoted to you. We
have nothing between us.'

'Nothing?' His laughter made it only too plain what he
thought of that. 'Lady, if this is nothing…'

His dark head came down fast and hard, those beautiful lips finding hers and clamping tight against her mouth,
crushing hers back against her teeth so that she could only
gasp in shocked response.

As a kiss it was cold and cruel, more like a punishment
than a caress, but appallingly it didn't matter. She didn't
care, couldn't think, could only feel. And the feeling that
was uppermost in her thoughts, pounding through her
body, was a raw hunger, a desperate need for this—and
so much more. She would have flung her hands up around
his neck, bringing his head down even closer, to deepen
and prolong that burning pressure, but the way he still
held her prevented that. She couldn't hold back and she

crushed her mouth against his, strained her body closer, feeling the heat and hardness of his erection that pushed against the cradle of her pelvis, telling her of his desire and feeding her own until she was swimming on a heated tide of longing, losing herself in him.

The moment when he broke off the kiss, snatched his mouth from hers, dropped her back down on to her feet—feet that she hadn't even been aware had left the floor—was like a brutal slap to her face. His name almost escaped her in a cry of shocked distress but she dragged her hands from his and flung them up and over her mouth to hold back the revealing sound.

'I think that showed you—showed both of us—how this will work. You say you don't know how to do this but it's so easy. I want you...'

Reaching out, he stroked a finger down the side of her cheek, watching intently as in spite of herself she shivered, her eyes closing in instinctive response.

'And I can have you if I want.'

That brought her eyes flying open again to stare, shocked, into his.

'No!'

He ignored her furious protest. 'Because you want me just as much. You responded. More than responded. You know as I do that if we'd been somewhere more private then things would have gone so much further.'

Breathing unevenly, he smoothed a hand over his face, brushed the other down his body to straighten the shirt her actions had creased, pulling it from his trousers at his waist.

'Perhaps it's best that things can't go any further now—before I do something that we'll both regret.'

'You've already done something I regret—something I wish had never happened!'

Was it the fact that it was a lie that made her voice so shrill? Or the way that her body was still struggling with the aftershocks of the reaction his kiss had sparked off in her, sparks fizzing along every nerve, burning up in her blood?

'Really? Then if that's the case, you'll not want this, either.'

She knew what was coming, and the tiny part of her mind that was still rational told her to step back, move away. Fast. But that tiny part was totally submerged in the burning flood of sensual need that swamped common sense, drowning it in the heat of the hunger that still throbbed deep inside. She saw the change in his eyes, the switch from ice to smoky shadows that matched her own mood, and her breath caught in her throat, her lips parting, ready for the very different kiss she knew he planned.

And the kiss she really wanted.

This time it was warm and gentle. It gave instead of taking. His mouth caressed hers, teased, tantalised, tempting it further open to allow the intimate invasion of his tongue. The cool, fresh taste of him was like a powerful aphrodisiac exploding against her lips, totally intoxicating, instantly addictive.

She melted into that kiss, almost swooning against him as the throb of desire took all the strength from her legs, made them feel like damp cotton wool beneath her. And when Alexei's arms came round her it only added to the sensual overload that had her at its mercy. The heat and scent of his body was like the burn of incense in her nostrils making her head swim.

This was the kiss she had always dreamed of, the kiss she had been waiting for all her life. The kiss she had once lain awake imagining long into the night as she felt the awakening of her female sexuality It was a kiss that made her know what it felt like to be a woman.

A woman who had found the man she wanted most in all of the world.

A woman who had discovered the man she…

Oh no! *No, no, no!*

Panic-stricken she froze, jerked back, tore herself away from him. What was she thinking? Where had that come from? How had she let that thought—that terrible, foolish, dangerous thought—creep into her mind?

Was she really so weak that she was allowing her adolescent self to resurface with all her foolish, gullible dreams, the fantasies she had indulged in when she couldn't face reality? The fictions she had created for herself when she had let herself pretend that perhaps one day, Alexei, the boy she had had such a heavyweight crush on, would turn to her and want her as a man would want a woman.

Well, yes, he wanted her now, there was no denying that. And she wanted him. He was right, he could have her if he wanted her. There was no way she was going to be able to resist him if he turned on the true high-octane power of his sensuality, the enticement of the seduction she knew he could channel without trying. But was she going to mistake the white-hot burn of adult sexuality for anything more?

This was the first real experience of true lust she had ever known and it seemed it had the power to burn away some much-needed brain cells, foolishly allowing her to confuse it with real feelings—emotions that her younger, naïve sense had once dreamed of knowing.

'No.'

Alexei had felt her withdrawal and his voice seemed to echo her thoughts, but so much more assuredly, calm and controlled—disturbingly so, considering the fires that had just blazed between them, the sparks that still seemed to sizzle in the air.

'No—we can't take this any further now.'

Shockingly he dropped another kiss on her upturned face. A brief, casual, almost affectionate kiss on her cheek. And the easiness of his response, the light-heartedness of his touch, rocked her even more than her own shattered thoughts of a moment before. They were kisses of certainty, relaxed, almost careless. The kisses of a man who knew that he could get exactly what he wanted—whenever he wanted—so that he didn't have to take too much trouble now.

'Too much to do. A reception committee outside.'

'Really?'

Knocked even more off-balance, Ria twisted on her heel, still within the confines of his arms, and bent slightly to look out the window.

Someone must have radioed ahead, informing the airport authorities—and more—of their planned arrival. And that someone must have announced not just that Alexei's private jet requested permission to land—but that Alexei Joachim Sarova, Crown Prince and future King of Mecjoria, was arriving back in his country, ready to take possession of the throne. There was a fleet of sleek black cars drawn up at the far side of the tarmac, smoked glass, bullet-proof windows, black bodyworks gleaming in the sun. A small Mecjorian flag fluttered on the bonnet of the lead vehicle and someone had rolled out a red carpet across the runway, leading to the bottom of the flight of steps that had now been brought to the door of the plane. A door that a member of the flight crew was hurrying to unlock, to let them out.

'We're here,' Alexei said. 'I'm here. This is what you wanted.'

What she wanted. He was going to make his claim for the throne; and that could only mean that he believed she had agreed to his conditions.

But why shouldn't he think that? Hadn't she given him every indication that she had accepted his terms—welcomed them if her response to his kiss was anything to go by?

After all, what other choice did she have? If she wanted Alexei to take the throne instead of Ivan then she had to go along with what he demanded of her. She had to marry him, become his queen. It was either that or marry Ivan, and the way that her blood ran cold at just the thought was enough to tell her that somewhere along the line she had decided to go along with Alexei's proposal even though she had no recollection of ever rationally doing so. She had no other possible alternative.

Turning back from the window, Alexei looked down into her face, dark eyes probing hers.

'We can make this work, Ria,' he said sombrely. 'Together we can do what's best for Mecjoria.'

Did he read anything else in her face? She would never know, but something made him pause, then go on to add, 'You're right that the royal family doesn't expect to marry for love—and I'm not offering that. I can't love you. I loved once—adored her... Lost her.'

Something darkened his face, his eyes. Something reaching out from the past and coiling round his memory, Ria realised as he went on.

Mariette. He meant Mariette, the dark-haired beauty who had been the mother of his child, who had had a total breakdown when the baby died and had ended up in a psychiatric hospital. Refusing ever to see him again.

'I'll never feel like that again. But as my queen you would be my equal. My consort. And I know you'll be a fine queen. How can you not when your father has trained you for this almost from the moment you were born?'

He must have known how the mention of her father would make her react because he waited as she tried to look away, to look anywhere but into his stunning face. Once again he touched her cheek very softly.

'We'll finish this later.'

It was his total assurance that terrified her. Particularly when she knew she had only herself to blame. Hadn't she practically flung herself into his arms like a sex-starved adolescent who had only been kissed for the very first time?

Well, yes, she wasn't going to deny the desire—the hunger—she felt when he kissed her. But knowing she wanted him was one thing, tying herself to him in the sort of cold-blooded dynastic marriage she had hoped to escape from totally another.

'Later…'

It was all that she could manage as someone knocked on the cabin door and she found herself released so swiftly that she stumbled backwards and away from him. The speed with which he discarded her and turned his attention to other matters, reaching for his jacket, shrugging it on, smoothing a hand over his hair, made her feel like some dirty little secret to be kept hidden away until he had time for her again. He had her cooperation in the bag, he believed, and now he wanted to focus on the reason why he was—why they were both—here.

Reaction setting in made her vision blur, her hands shake, as she collected her own coat and her bag. She couldn't look at Alexei, couldn't bear to see the dark certainty, the satisfaction that she knew must show on his face. She wanted to get out of here, get her feet back down on the ground in more ways than one.

As she reached the door of the plane she was ahead of him. Just a couple of steps but enough. In the doorway at the top of the steps she suddenly realised, all her training kicking in, so that she hesitated, stopped. Reality hit home with the truth of who he now was. Carefully she took that couple of steps back and out of the way.

'Sir,' she said, resisting the urge to drop a curtsey even if only to defy him, to prove that he might have her in a cleft stick, but she wasn't going down without a fight. She was still her own woman and she would hang on to that for as long as she could.

She saw that elegant mouth twitch slightly, curling at the corners in a way that told her he knew only too well what was in her mind and a brief inclination of his head acknowledged everything unspoken that had passed between them. A moment later he was past her, standing in the doorway, looking down at the reception committee waiting for him, before stepping out into the warmth of the evening air.

As he went down the steps to the tarmac with cameras flashing like wild lightning in the distance, warning them of what was to come, what was inevitable now that the prodigal prince had come home, she spotted one moment when he paused, just for the space of a heartbeat, and squared his shoulders like a man accepting his destiny and going to meet his future. He hadn't wanted this, she recalled. He had practically thrown her out of his house when she had first put the proposition to him. Whatever else she might think of him, she could see that unlike Ivan, who wanted the crown for the prestige, the power, and of course the huge wealth that came with it,

Alexei appeared to have totally different reasons for going ahead with this.

Together we can do what's best for Mecjoria.

Whatever else was between them was personal—*this* was for the country's future. And at least on that she and Alexei were in agreement. But it—with her involvement—had taken away his freedom, the life he had lived up to now. His existence would never be the same again, and knowing the position she was in now, with her own freedom given up to secure peace for the country, Ria felt she understood that on a much deeper level than when she had got on a plane here at this same airport to go and try to persuade him to do just this.

So when he paused at the foot of the step, stopping before he actually set foot on Mecjorian land—his country—she spotted it at once. She was there so close behind him that they were almost touching, his sudden hesitation making her almost slam into him from behind. And when he half-turned, dark eyes meeting hers just for a moment, and he held out his hand to her, she moved forward quickly, putting her fingers into his without hesitation or uncertainty. She felt the power of his touch close round her, holding firm and strong, and welcomed it as she walked down beside him, stepping onto Mecjorian soil together.

It was only when she looked back at that moment later, when it was played over and over on national TV, seeing it from the view of the reception committee of government ministers and army top brass lined up beside the red carpet waiting to greet Alexei, that she saw it properly. Saw how clearly it demonstrated that she had made her choice even before she had actually done so rationally within her own thoughts. That she had cast in her lot with Alexei, and without ever saying so had agreed to the future that he had decreed for both of them.

CHAPTER NINE

TOGETHER.

The word seemed to have taken up permanent residence inside Ria's head, mocking her with the memories of the day they had arrived in Mecjoria and the thoughts she had let herself consider then.

Together. She had let herself believe that Alexei had meant that there was a together in all this. That she and Alexei were working to the same ends. That her role as his fiancée might mean that she would actually be by his side, that they could be partners in this.

That he might actually need her just a little bit.

But it seemed that, having announced their engagement and presented her to the court, to the country, as his prospective bride, he had lost interest. There had been the moment when they had set foot on the red carpet, when the army officers, the dignitaries, had moved forward, bowed, saluted, address him as 'Your Majesty' and she had known that this was after all coming true.

Then Alexei had acknowledged their greetings, shaken hands, all the time holding on to hers so tightly that his grip felt like a manacle around her wrist. She had had to move with him; it was either that or create an ugly little scene as she tried to break away. She had to endure the fusillade of camera flashes, the frankly curious and as-sessing stares of everyone who was there—the ones who knew of her father's fall from grace, his imprisonment, her own loss of any title and status at the court as a result.

And then, at last, just before they headed for the waiting cars, Alexei had finally announced the reason why she was there.

'Gentlemen,' he had said in a voice that carried clear and strong in spite of the wicked breeze that was swirling round them now. 'Let me present to you my fiancée— and future queen—the Grand Duchess Honoria Maria Escalona…'

And with that her place in all this was fixed, settled once and for all. Her title it seemed was restored to her, her place in society reinstated. But she was trapped even more tightly in the web of intrigue and plotting that had created this situation in the first place. The speed and conviction with which it had happened made her head spin.

But once they were back in Mecjoria it seemed that everything she had been anticipating hadn't happened. Nothing might have changed for all the difference it made in her relationship with Alexei. He didn't even seem to want her sexually any more. She had been convinced that he would press home the advantage he'd made it clear he knew he had while they were on the plane. But it appeared that as soon as he had her on his side for the future of Mecjoria and had introduced her as his fiancée, so putting her firmly in the limelight and in the place he wanted her at his side, he seemed to have lost interest.

She had been settled in a beautiful suite in the huge, golden-stoned palace high on the hill above the capital. A far more beautiful and luxurious suite than she had ever enjoyed on her rare visits there in the past. Her clothes, her personal belongings, had been brought from her home and delivered to her room, and she had been left to settle in.

Alone.

Later she had been sent a series of instructions—details of where she was expected to be and when. There were dinners, receptions, public appearances. There had been a whole new wardrobe provided for these events too with visits from top couturiers, fittings for every sort of dress, shoes, jewellery imaginable. She was now dressed more glamorously than ever in life before. But then she was used to this. It was how it had always been with her father. What was different was the way that, once he had let her know where she was to be, Alexei left everything else up to her. Her father had wanted more control than that. For each event she had been given a series of commands disguised as strict guidelines, as to what she was to do, when she was to appear, what she was to wear, the subjects she should read up on in order to be able to talk about. Alexei made no such demands; and she valued the confidence, the trust, he put in her that way.

She had performed her duty at Alexei's side, smiled when she needed to, made polite, careful conversation with everyone she was introduced to, walked with her hand on his arm, eaten the meals put in front of her. She had executed her role of the apparently devoted fiancée to perfection, and then returned to her room.

Alone.

But there had been one special duty that he had entrusted to her. One that he felt that she was the best person in the country to carry out.

'We need to broadcast the story of the discovery of the proof of my parents' marriage,' he told her. 'Everyone is asking questions, making up the most impossible stories.'

Between them, they had come up with a version that came close enough to the truth. A story that involved the missing document being discovered in some long-unopened files. There was no need to detail Ria's father's involvement in it, Alexei had conceded, obviously not wanting his new fiancée's name blackened by any connection with Gregor's plotting.

'You'll be able to get close enough to the truth when you say how you discovered it, and it will explain why you came to England to contact me,' he told her as he escorted her to the TV studios from which she was to broadcast the details the press wanted.

She knew it was all show, just part of the masquerade they were putting on, but all the same she hugged to herself a feeling of delight at the way that Alexei left her to herself to decide what to say and how to say it. She knew he was watching in the background, scrutinising every move she made, but he had trusted her and that was what mattered. And at the end of the interview, when all the cameras were turned off, he had put his hand on her shoulder, drawing her close to drop a kiss on to her cheek.

'Thank you,' he had said quietly, his breath warm on her skin. 'The mention of the way that your visit to London meant we had the chance to renew our friendship from when we were here in Mecjoria all those years ago was inspired. It was just what was needed.'

Ria nodded agreement, swallowing down the way that 'friendship' covered such a multitude of sins. 'And with any luck the romance story will grab the headlines more.'

Her instincts proved right. The 'fairy-tale romance' between the new king and the daughter of one of the oldest families in Mecjoria was what caught the headlines. For every appearance Alexei made on his own, the interest was trebled if the two of them were seen together. The flash and crash of cameras on every occasion was like an assault, and the coverage in every newspaper made it seem as if there was no other subject under the sun.

Alexei hadn't allowed her to make any contact with her family. Her mother might have packed up her clothes for delivery to the castle, and she had included a brief note, just a card, to thank Ria for her success in bringing Alexei to Mecjoria, but that was all. And nothing more was allowed, it seemed. There might be murmurs of curiosity as to where Ria's father could be, but as her mother was known to be ill and had retired to the family's country house to recover it was rarely taken any further than a comment. And when it was, then the next walkabout by the 'fairy tale' couple pushed the query well away from the front page. Her family would be in touch, there would be news about her father, when the time was right, Ria was told.

But when would the time be right?

She had never managed to snatch more than a few moments' conversation with the man she was engaged to and even those were necessarily casual and uncontroversial because of their public setting, with hundreds of listeners in to every word they said, a phalanx of photographers lined up to record their every move. At the end of the day Alexei would smile, give her a kiss on both cheeks, one more on her mouth that their audience was waiting for, and walk away, back to the council rooms or his office, to discuss the next steps in the preparation for the coronation, leaving her alone.

And wanting more.

He might be able to switch off so completely, to concentrate on what mattered most to him—but she couldn't. She spent long, sleepless nights alone in the huge soft bed in the luxurious gold and white room, unable to settle. She was lonely, side-lined—frustrated. It was too painful a reminder of how she had once felt, all those years before, when she had been just an adolescent and she hadn't truly understood what these feelings were, where they came from. Now she was a grown woman, experiencing adult feelings for an adult male, and she knew exactly what they meant.

She wanted him. In every way that a woman wanted a man. She wanted him in her life, in her bed…inside her body. So much so that she ached now just thinking of it. Sighing, Ria tossed and turned, hunger buzzing along her nerves. She had never thought when she had agreed to go and find Alexei, talk to him, that she would open this whole Pandora's Box of memories. She had thought that she could face him as an adult, face down the hurt of past times. That she could persuade him to set her country free from the threats that surrounded it, and put herself on to a new path into the future as a result.

Instead she had thrown herself into a whole new volcano of sensual reaction, taken the lid off a set of feelings that, developed and matured by time, were now too big, too powerful to ever go quietly back into the box no matter how hard she tried.

But had she got it so terribly wrong? Was the truth that he was using her, using the desire she had been unable to hide, to make her do as he said, act in the way that benefitted him most? She had been manoeuvred into this position, playing the role of his fiancée, only to be frozen out on any more personal level. So was she really just a pawn in the game of dynastic chess he had set out to play with the country's future—and with hers? Just a way to cement his position as king or did he want something more from her?

'Oh why do I have to feel this way? Still!'

Turning restlessly on fine linen sheets that suddenly seemed as rough as cheap polyester against her sensitised skin, Ria pummelled her pillow, desperately trying to find a comfortable spot that might help her relax. Outside, the dark of the night was filled with a heavy, oppressive warmth, the low, rumble of thunder circling against the mountains and across the valley towards the castle. The long voile curtains waved in the breeze, as restless and unsettled as her thoughts. But it wasn't the heat outside that made her body burn but the flare of feelings deep inside.

Alexei had declared openly that he would never love her, but she had thought that he had responded to her at least as a woman. That he had wanted her as much as she did him. She had told herself that she wouldn't ask for more. She hadn't thought that she might have to settle for so much less.

Knowing that sleep was impossible, Ria tossed back the bedclothes, swinging her feet to the floor and reaching for the pale blue robe that lay at the foot of the bed, a match for the beautiful silk nightdress she was wearing.

When it had been delivered, along with the other new outfits she was expected to wear for her official duties, she had thought that there was perhaps a secret message in the garments. That they were meant for the time when she and Alexei would get together and finish what they had started in London and later on the plane journey here. She had waited six long nights, the pretty blue nightgown had become crumpled with wear. But not any more.

'Six nights is long enough!'

She wasn't going to sit here any longer like some unwanted spare part. She wasn't thirteen any more, trained to be compliant, doing as her father said.

She didn't even have to do as Alexei said; not unless she wanted to.

Tightening the belt of the blue robe around her waist and pushing her feet into soft white slippers, she marched towards the door and flung it open.

'Madame?'

The instant response, in a quiet, respectful male voice, startled her. She had forgotten that Alexei had warned her of the need for security following the unrest that had resulted from the problems over the accession to the throne. Drawing herself up hastily, she directed a cool gaze at the security officer.

'His Majesty asked to see me.'

'Of course, madame. If you'll just follow me…'

The problem was, Ria acknowledged to herself as he led her down long high-ceilinged corridors, that now she was committed. How would this man react if she suddenly declared that she wasn't going to obey the summons she had claimed after all?

But they had reached their destination before she had time to think things through, her guide stopping by another huge carved wooden door, rapping lightly on it and then standing back with a swift, neat bow.

'Yes?'

The door was yanked open and Alexei stood in the doorway, tall and devastating, more imposing than ever.

He had discarded the dinner jacket he'd had on earlier that evening but he still wore the immaculate white shirt, now pulled open at the throat with his black bow tie, tugged loose and left dangling around his neck. His hair was in ruffled disarray, as if he had been running his hands through it again and again, and he held a crystal tumbler with some clear liquid swirling about at the bottom of it.

'Madame Duchess…'

His voice was dark with cynicism, no warmth of welcome in it.

Without thinking, Ria reverted to the formality of etiquette she had been trained in and dipped into a neat curtsey, holding the blue skirts of her robe out around her as if they were some formal ball gown.

'You asked to see me, sir.'

I did? She could see the question in his eyes, the way the straight black brows snapped together in astonishment, but luckily his sharp jet gaze went to the man behind her and obviously caught on. He nodded and stepped back, opening the door even wider.

'I did, duchess,' he responded with a grave formality that was at odds with the twitch of the corners of his mouth. 'Come in.'

It took all Ria's control to move forward, walk past the security guard and into the room. Just at the last moment she recovered enough composure to turn and switch on a swift, controlled smile.

'Thank you,' she murmured.

Then she was inside and the door was closed behind her, leaving her alone with Alexei.

This suite was larger even than the one she had spent the last week in. Huge rooms, vast windows, decorated in shades of dark green. But now, seeing it with him standing beside her, she couldn't help recalling the building she had seen him in in London. Here, the stiff formality of the décor, the furnishings in the dark heavy wood, made it look as if it had been decorated twenty years or more before. There were no photographs here, she noticed, recalling how those elegant but somehow cold, isolated—lonely—images had hit home the first time she had seen them. In fact there was nothing personal here, nothing of Alexei. Only the new king.

Ria managed another couple of steps into the room, then slowed, stopped, as the full force of the scene outside the door hit home.

'Oh dear heaven…' Even she couldn't tell if her voice

shook with laughter or embarrassment. 'Henri. What he must have thought!'

'And what was that?' Alexei drawled, taking a sip of his drink.

'That you— He must have thought that you had summoned me to your room…'

She couldn't complete the sentence but the dark gleam in Alexei's eyes told her that he had followed her thought processes exactly.

'And would it have been so very terrible if I had? Why should you not be in my room? We are engaged to be married, after all. And from the stories of our romance in the press, everyone will be expecting that we are already lovers.'

The last of his drink was tossed to the back of his throat, swallowed hard. Ria watched every last inch of its progress down the lean bronzed length of his throat, almost to the point where the first evidence of crisp, dark body hair showed at the neck of his white shirt. Compulsively she found herself matching the movement, though her own gulping swallow did nothing to ease the heated dryness of her mouth.

'That being so, they probably wondered why you haven't been here before. So tell me—to what do I owe the honour of this visit?'

What had seemed so totally right when she had been tossing and turning in her bed, her body on fire with longing, now seemed impossible. The restless hunger hadn't eased—if anything, standing here like this so close to the living, breathing reality of her dreams, able to see the gleam of health on the golden skin, the lustre of his black hair, smell the personal scent of his body, made it all so much worse, much more visceral and primitive. But how could she come right out and *say* it?

'Perhaps I feel the way the paparazzi feel...'

His frown revealed his confusion and perhaps a touch of disbelief.

'I want to know more than just what event I'm attending, what dress I'll be wearing. I'm wondering just what I'm doing here—why you have me imprisoned.'

It was the first thing that came to her mind—and the worst, it seemed. Danger flared in his eyes, and the glass he held slammed down on a nearby table.

'Not imprisoned! You are free to come and go as you please.'

'Oh perhaps not like my father, I agree. I'm your fiancée—we're supposed to be getting married but that's almost as much as I know. I need to know just what I'm doing here.'

I need to know what we can do to make this work, she added in her own thoughts but totally lost the nerve to actually say the words aloud.

CHAPTER TEN

'Oh come now, Ria,' Alexei mocked. 'You know only too well why you are here. I want you—and you want me. We have only to look at each other and we go up in flames.'

Right now she felt that that was exactly the truth. The moment of cold had vanished and now the surface of her skin seemed to be burning up. When he prowled nearer she had to clench her hands in the skirts of her nightdress and robe, keeping them prisoner and away from the dangerous impulse to reach out and touch him.

'So much so that you haven't even been near me!' she scorned. 'You've sent me jewels—flowers.'

'I thought women liked flowers—and jewellery.'

Ria batted the interruption aside with a wave of her fingers then snatched her hand back again as if stung as skin met skin where it had accidentally brushed his cheek. She could feel the wave of colour rising in her cheeks as she saw the way his eyes darkened in instant response, sending her body temperature rocketing skywards.

'And you look beautiful in that nightdress,' he continued, unrepressed.

'So beautiful that ever since we came back to Mecjoria you have barely spent a day in my company.'

'Are you saying that you've been missing me?' Alexei questioned with sudden softness.

Missing you so badly that it's eating me up inside.

'I am supposed to be your fiancée!' she flung back.

Alexei's slow smile mocked the vehemence of her response.

'And right now you are doing a wonderful job of sounding exactly like the jealous fiancée I would like you to be.'

'Jealous of what—who?'

'Of the time I spend with my new mistresses.'

It took her several moments to realise exactly what he meant. Not real women but the demands of the kingdom, the affairs of state.

'It was inevitable that you would be so occupied in these first days,' she acknowledged. 'You have so much to do. But you were wrong, you know, you didn't need any help.'

She had been impressed at the way he had taken charge since they had returned to Mecjoria. She'd watched him go through all the ceremony, the diplomatic meetings, seen the calm dignity and strength with which he'd conducted himself. He'd handled everyone, from the highest nobility to the ordinary commoner, with grace and ease.

'You've done wonderfully well—never put a foot wrong.'

A slight inclination of his head acknowledged the compliment which had been nothing less than the truth.

'I had a good teacher.'

Now it was her turn to frown. But then her expression changed abruptly as she met his eyes.

'I've done nothing,' she protested.

'The people want to see you,' Alexei countered. 'They love you and so do the press.'

'It's the Romeo and Juliet element—our "romance"—' She broke off abruptly as he shook his head almost savagely.

'You've been at my side every day. You're a link to the old monarchy and you've lived in Mecjoria all your life. People value that.'

Was he saying that he valued it too? Her heart ached to know the answer to that question.

'Who else could I ask this of other than someone like you?' His hand cupped her cheek, dark eyes looking down into hers in a way that somehow made this so personal between the two of them, not just a matter of state. 'Someone who loves Mecjoria, who belongs here.'

'You belong here now!'

Too late she heard that 'now' fall into a dangerous silence. One that came with too many memories, too much darkness attached to it. And she knew that he felt that way too when his hand fell away, breaking the fragile contact between them.

'I know you never wanted to come back to Mecjoria.'

'Ah, but there you couldn't be more wrong,' Alexei put in sharply. 'Why do you think I was so furious when we got thrown out? Why I hated what had happened to us? This was my father's homeland. I wanted to be accepted here. To belong here. And I grew to love the country-side—the lakes, the mountains.'

His eyes went to the windows where in the daylight those mountains could be seen, rising majestically against the horizon, so high that they were always capped with a layer of snow, even in the summer.

'That was what got me hooked on photography. I wanted to capture the stunning beauty of Alabria. The wildlife in the forests. It was my father who gave me my first camera. That was the one thing I managed to take with me into exile.'

Exile. That single word spoke of so much more. Of love and loss and loneliness. Particularly when she was remembering those photographs on the walls of his office. The ones that had made him his fortune, built his reputation. Their stylised bleakness could not have been in starker contrast to the gentle beauty of the forests and lakes, the animals that had first made him want to capture their images.

'Do you still have that camera?'

He didn't use words to answer her. Instead he gestured to a heavy wooden chest of drawers that stood against the wall. Only now did Ria see the well-worn leather camera case that stood on top of it, its plain and battered appearance at odds with the old-fashioned ornate décor of the rest of the room. Her heart clenched, making her catch her breath.

'Your father would have been proud of you.'

Something in what she had said made his mouth, which had relaxed for a moment, twist tightly, cynically.

'*Now,*' he said roughly. 'He would have felt very differently about the son he had while he was still alive.'

'You didn't exactly get a chance.' Honesty forced her to say it. 'The court is hidebound by archaic rules and protocols. They can take years to learn if you haven't grown up getting used to them. And it was so much worse ten years ago. Even now it's bad enough.'

Alexei's smile was wry, almost boyish, reminding her sharply of so many occasions from the past. 'And have you any idea how many times I've checked you out at some moment this week when I've needed to know exactly what the protocol was?'

'You have?' She had never noticed that. And the fact that he would admit to it stunned her.

'Like I said—I've had a good teacher.'

'I wish I'd done more in the past. I could have helped you then.'

'Your father made sure you had no opportunity for that,' he commented cynically. 'He had his plans for you even then and nothing was going to get in the way. Particularly not some jumped-up commoner from an inconvenient marriage he had thought was long forgotten.'

'You think that even then…?'

She fought against the nausea rising in her throat. It was worse than she thought.

'I know.'

Alexei's nod was like a hammer blow on any hopes that things were not as bad as she had feared. A death blow to the dream that Alexei would not want to take the revenge that he was justified in seeking.

'If it had not been Ivan, it would have been someone else. Whoever offered him the greatest chance at being the power behind the throne.'

'Anyone but you.' It was just a whisper.

'Anyone but me.'

And there it was. The real reason why she was here. What was it people said—don't ask the question if you can't take the answer? She'd asked and so she had only herself to blame if the answer was not what she wanted to hear. And how could she want to hear that her place at Alexei's side, the link to the old monarchy she brought with her, provided the perfect revenge for all that Gregor had ever done to this man, the inheritance he had deprived him of? The father. The homeland.

'Tell me.' Alexei's voice seemed to come from a long way away. 'Could you really have married Ivan?'

Even for the country? She had once thought that she could but now, in the darkness of the night, she couldn't suppress the shudder that shook her at just the thought.

That was why her father was still in jail, Alexei acknowledged privately as he watched the colour drain

from her face. All the investigations he had carried out
since returning to Mecjoria had only proved even further
just what sort of a slippery, devious cold fish Gregor Escalona still was. The man who had plotted his downfall
and his mother's ruin would sell his soul to the devil if the
price was right. He was not about to let the bastard out of
jail until he was sure that he had control of him in other
ways. And that control came through Escalona's daughter. With Ria at his side, as his wife, he had an unassailable claim to the throne. Surely even Gregor would think
twice about staging a palace revolution when it would
harm his daughter?

Though even that was something he still couldn't be
sure of. Gregor had always been a cold and neglectful
father. That was one of the reasons why Ria had sought
out his friendship back in the past. They had been—he'd
thought—two lost and lonely youngsters caught in the
heartless world of power struggles and conspiracies. The
sort of conspiracy in which Gregor had shown himself to
be quite prepared to use his daughter to his own advantage. Signing the treaty with Ivan was evidence of that.

Which was why he had to marry Ria—*another* reason
why he had to marry her, he admitted. He wasn't going
to let Escalona near her until she was truly his wife. Only
then could he protect her from being forced to marry Ivan
in any counter-revolution to gain the crown. It was the
thought of her married to Ivan that had pushed him into
the proposal from the start—but now the thought that she
might have been pressured into marrying a man she so
obviously feared reinforced that already steel-hard resolve
to make her his queen.

Whatever else Gregor had done wrong, the way he had
raised his daughter had prepared her so well for the role
she would fulfil. He had been sure she would be an asset

to his claim to the throne and she had proved herself in so many ways.

But of course they weren't married yet. And until they were he wasn't going to let Escalona anywhere near his daughter.

But when an ugly little question was raised inside his head, demanding to know just what made him any different from the bullying father who would have pushed her into a forced marriage without considering her feelings, he was uncomfortably aware of the fact that he didn't have an answer to give, not one that would satisfy even himself.

'And marrying me?' he demanded roughly.

A small flick of her head might have been an answer. It might just as well have been a dismissal of the question as one she refused to answer. Her lips were pressed tight against each other, as if refusing to let any real response out. The problem was the deep gut-instinct that wrenched at him, seeing that. He wanted to lean forward, to stroke his thumb along the line of her mouth, ease those rose-tinted lips apart, cover her mouth with his, taste her, invade the moist warmth.

His heart thudded so hard against his rib cage that he felt sure she must hear it and his body hardened in hunger that made him want to groan aloud. When he had chosen that blue nightdress and robe he had imagined how she might look in it, the pale silk and darker blue lace contrasting with the creamy softness of her skin; the deep vee neckline plunging over the smooth curves of her breasts, the rich tumble of her hair along her shoulders. The reality far overshadowed his imaginings and his senses were even further besieged by the perfume of some floral shampoo as she moved her head, the scent of her skin driving him half-crazy with sexual need.

'That's a *fait accompli.*' Ria's cool voice sliced into his heated imaginings, making him fight to pay attention to what she was actually saying. 'But don't you think our "romance" will be more convincing if we spend more time together—as a man and a woman, not just as king and queen? I appreciate that you have many commitments—duties. Though I would have thought that when those duties were done...'

'You'd have liked me to come to your room, to snatch an hour—maybe less?' he challenged. 'You would have thought that was worth it?'

If he'd gone to her room then he wouldn't have stayed just for an hour, that was the truth. If he'd visited her there once, they would never have emerged until both of them were sated and exhausted. And he would have been totally in her power, sexually enslaved as never before in his life. He wasn't ready to risk that yet. He had the disturbing feeling that it would not be enough. That he would never be free again.

'I would have liked some attention—other than these *gifts!*'

'You don't like presents?'

'Presents are not...'

Ria almost choked on the realisation of what she had been about to say. Presents are not feelings. Presents are not *love*. Just where had that word come from?

Love. She didn't want to think that. She most definitely didn't want to feel that. But, now that the word had slipped into her thoughts, there was no way she was going to get it back into its box.

'Presents are not...?' Alexei prompted when she found her tongue frozen, unable to continue.

'Not important.' She bit the words out.

'A pity.' It actually sounded genuine. 'I had hoped you

would enjoy them. So perhaps I should cancel tomorrow's sessions with the couturier?'

'What would I need *more* dresses for? I have more than—'

'For the Black and White Ball,' Alexei inserted smoothly, cutting her off. There was a new glint in his eyes and his mouth seemed to have softened unexpectedly. 'You didn't think I would go ahead with that?' he asked as he saw the astonishment she couldn't hide. 'It is tradition. And you always wanted to attend such an event.'

She'd told him that when she was thirteen. Ten years ago. And he'd remembered?

'With the masks and everything?'

She couldn't stop the excitement from creeping into her voice. She had always been fascinated by the black and white masked ball that was traditionally held to mark the start of the coronation celebrations. The last time it had happened she had been too young to attend, and the sudden and unexpected death of the new king had come before there had been time to organise it.

'With the masks,' Alexei confirmed.

'I never expected that you of all people would be interested.'

'Me of all people?'

Another mistake. His mood had changed totally, taking with it the lighter atmosphere that had touched the room.

'And why is that, my dear duchess? Did you think that a commoner like me would not be able to cope with a formal ball?'

'I never…' She had been thinking of his wild past, the stories in the papers of long sessions in nightclubs, the images of him emerging, bleary-eyed and dishevelled, in the early hours of the morning. That terrible photo of him battered and bruised, his face bloody. 'I didn't think it would be your sort of thing.'

'I can dance. My father insisted that I had lessons—it's not something I'm likely to forget.'

There was such a wealth of memory in that statement that it woke echoes in Ria's mind.

'Madame Herone?' she questioned, recalling the hours she had spent being drilled in ballroom dancing by the stern disciplinarian.

Alexei nodded, that gleam deepening in the darkness of his eyes.

'I'm surprised we didn't end up having lessons together.'

No, she'd overstepped some mark there, she realised, feeling a painful twist of regret as the warmth faded like an ebbing tide.

'Your father was determined that we should never spend time together.'

She hadn't known that. Had simply believed that the dance lessons, like so many other things, were something that Alexei had rebelled against. How many other stories had she been told that had been just that—lies told to prevent her getting too close to him, getting to know him properly?

'It might have made everything so much more bearable. Do you remember that cane she had?'

Ria shuddered as she remembered how the dance teacher had wielded the cane like a weapon, rapping it sharply and painfully against her pupils' ankles if they made a mistake.

'I used to come out of lessons with my legs a mass of bruises.'

'No Huh-Honoria…' Alexei's tone mimicked the teacher's delivery perfectly, with a strange half-breath before her name. 'On your toes, if you please… And one, two, three—one, two, three…'

He was holding out his arms to Ria as he spoke and she found herself moving into them, picking up the rhythm.

'*One,* two, three…'

The speed was building. She was being swung around, whirled about the room, faster and faster. And she was being held so close, his arm at her back, clamped against the base of her spine, crushing her against him so that she could feel the heat of his body through the fine silk of her nightdress. Not just the heat; crushed this close, she couldn't be unaware of the hardness and power of his erection that spoke of a deeper, more primitive need than the light-hearted dance he had lead her into. Her feet barely seemed to touch the floor, her toes lifting from the carpet as she was steered across the room.

But it wasn't just the speed of the dance or the whirling turns that made her head spin. It was the sensation of being held in his arms, their strength supporting her, the burn of his palm at her back where the nightgown dipped low over her spine. His heartbeat, heavy, powerful, strong just under her cheek, seemed to take her pulse and lift it, make it throb in an unconscious echo of his, her breathing quickening, become shallow.

'One, two, three…'

She would never know if it was an accident or deliberate but at that moment it seemed that his foot caught on the edge of a rug, throwing them off-balance, stumbling, falling. Somehow Alexei twisted so that she landed safely on to the huge soft bed, crushed a heartbeat later by the heavy weight of Alexei's long body.

'Alex!' His name escaped on a rush of air, gasping in a mix of complicated reactions.

With her face buried against the strong column of his

neck, nose against the warm satin of his skin, she could inhale the personal scent of his body, feel the effect of it slide through her like warm smoke. If she just pushed her lips forward a centimetre or less she would taste him, be able to press her tongue against the lean muscles, the heavy pulse.

Above her Alexei went totally still, freezing into an immobility that caught the breath in her throat and held it there, tightly knotted.

'Ria,' he said, rough and raw as if dragged from a painfully sore throat. 'Ria, look at me...'

Half-fearful, half-excited, she made herself look up at him, meeting the gleaming onyx blaze of his eyes and feeling it burning up inside her. His face was set and raw, skin stretched tight across his broad cheekbones where a flash of red stained them darkly. She knew what that meant, knew her own face must bear a similar mark. Her blood was molten in her veins, her heartbeat thundering at her temples so that she couldn't think straight.

'*This* is why I never came to you before now. I knew that if I came to you it would be like this.'

He moved slightly, stroking a warm palm over her exposed skin, shifting against her so that she felt the heated swell of his erection. The heady mix of excitement and hunger drove her to make a soft mewling sound that had him drawing in a raw, unsteady breath.

'I knew that I would never get away again.'

He shook his dark head roughly, closing his eyes against the admission that had been dragged from him. Pushing both hands into the drift of her hair across the pillows, he held her head just so, dark eyes fixing hers, his mouth just a few centimetres of temptation away from her own.

'I didn't want to want you so much—never did. But

there is little point in denying it any more. So now, my duchess, it is decision time. If you are going to say no then say it now—while I can still act on it.'

Bending his head, he took her lips in a kiss that was pure temptation, sliding into a hungry pressure that told its own story. It was barely there then gone again and the moan of disappointment that rose in her throat, the way that her own mouth followed his, trying to snatch back the caress, made it plain that she wanted more. The hands that had been in her hair now slid down the length of her body, one cupping her bottom and pressing her closer against him, the other slipping under the lace-trimmed edge of the blue silk gown, sliding it from her shoulder, baring the creamy skin to his mouth.

The heat of his kiss made her writhe on the dark green covers, and when his teeth grazed her skin in a tender pain another soft cry of response escaped her.

Six restless nights had brought her to his door. Six nights of wakefulness and frustration, six nights of longing and growing need. And every one of those nights was behind her action now. She was hungry, needy, her hands shaking as she pulled at his clothes, wrenching his shirt from the waistband of his trousers, tugging it up so that she had access to the smooth warmth of the skin of his back. With the other hand, she reached up, catching the dangling ends of his unfastened bow tie and holding them together, pulling down on them to draw his head towards her, his mouth imprisoned against her own, his groan escaping from between their joined lips.

She was lost in those kisses, abandoned to his touch. His hands were even more impatient than her own, dispensing with the fine blue silk that covered her with a roughness and a lack of finesse that had the fine material ripping as he tore it away from her. And then his mouth was on her breast, hot and hungry, kissing, nipping, suckling in a way that brought a moaning response from her own throat.

'Lexei...' she sobbed, daring at last to use again the affectionate nickname he had once let her call him. 'Lexei...'

A sudden thought seemed to catch him, making him pause, lift his head.

'You're not...?'

'What? A virgin?' Ria finished for him, the fight she was having to cope with this abrupt change making her tone sharp, the words shake on her tongue. 'What—do you think I spent all these years just waiting, saving myself for you? Don't be silly.'

She might just as well have done, she added in the privacy of her own thoughts. She had believed herself in love with Alexei, had had fantasies, dreams in which he had been the one—her first. So when he had left and had made it plain that he had never spared a thought for the former friend he had left behind, when he had been seen everywhere with the beautiful, glamorous Mariette, when he had had a baby with the other woman, she had later flung herself into a relationship at the age of twenty that she'd known within days had been a major mistake. And if she had needed any further proof then it was right here, right now in the storm of feelings breaking over her. The sort of tempest that no other person had ever been able to arouse in her.

The nightdress was gone, ripped away and discarded on the floor, and somehow he had managed to shed his own clothes, the heat and hair-roughened texture of his skin a torment of delight against her own sensitised flesh. And when he combined it with the stinging delight of his hot mouth closing over one pouting nipple she could only throw back her head against the pillows and choke his name out loud.

When he threw a leg over hers, pushing her thighs apart, opening her to him, she went with him willingly, arching up to meet him, to encourage him, to welcome him. With her face muffled against his throat she slid her hands down to his buttocks and pressed hard, urging him on.

'Ria…' Her name was rough and thick on his tongue, revealing that if she was on the brink of losing control then he was right there with her all the way. His mouth was at one breast, his hands teasing the other, tugging at her nipple, drawing it tighter, and she thought that she might lose the little that was left of her consciousness as she felt her head swim with the sensual pleasure that was burning up inside her.

The moment that he eased himself inside her had her holding her breath, abandoning herself, yielding herself up to him. The slow slide of his body into hers was like that teenage dream come true but harder, hotter, so much more than she had ever been able to imagine in her fantasies. It went beyond any experience that she could have ever thought was possible.

She was so close to the edge already that there was barely time to breathe between this moment of intense connection and the pulse of something new, something hot and hungry and demanding as he moved within her, and she lifted herself to meet his thrusts, gasping her delight as they took her higher, higher…soaring into the heavens, it seemed.

A moment later she was lost. Sensations stormed every inch of her body, assaulting every nerve, her mind whirling in the delirium of ecstasy. She froze with her body arched up to his, her internal muscles clamping around him so that she caught his choking cry of release as he too let go and abandoned himself to the tidal wave of pleasure, losing himself in the oblivion of fulfilment.

The storm of sensual ecstasy that had exploded inside Alexei's head took a long time to recede. Even then, it was impossible to move, impossible to think. His heart thundered against his ribs and it seemed his breathing would never get back under control. But at long last the red-hot tide receded, his blood cooled, his mind was his own again. With Ria's soft warmth curled up close beside him, her face buried against his chest, her hair spilling across his arms, he knew a powerful sense of satisfaction, of the closest thing to contentment he had known in a long time.

A contentment that was shattered in the moment that the first rational thought invaded his mind like a shaft of ice.

What the hell had he done?

He had known that he had kept away from Ria for a reason. The reason being that he didn't trust his own control when he was with her. He wanted her but, after the bitter lesson he had learned in the past, he had vowed that never again would he risk sleeping with any woman without contraception. But the moment Ria had been in his arms, the heat of the hunger he had felt as she lay underneath him, open to him, giving to him, had taken all his ability to think and shattered it. He hadn't even had a brain cell working that had thought of protection or consequences or the future. Only here and now and what was happening between them.

In a lifetime of wild, reckless, foolish mistakes, he might just have made the worst possible one ever.

CHAPTER ELEVEN

RIA STARED AT her reflection in the mirror and tried to recognise herself in the woman she saw there. The change wasn't just physical, though the groomed, elegant person who looked back at her was so far from any previous image of herself she had ever seen. There was so much more to it than that. And that meant that she found it hard to look herself in the eye, harder to admit to what she was seeing there.

Her dress was perfection, the sort of dress she might have imagined in her dreams. A narrow, strapless column of white silk, it had tiny crystals stitched into the material so that the effect when she moved was like a fall of stars. Her hair was swept into an elegant half-up, half-down style with the rich glowing strands falling over the creamy skin of her shoulders and partway down her back.

Growing up, she had always dreamed about one day being able to attend the black and white masked ball. She had also dreamed of falling in love, of marrying and living her own happy ever after. And the biggest part of that dream had been loving just one man.

Loving Alexei Sarova.

Well, she had done just that. She'd given him her heart as a child, but now she'd fallen in love with him for real, as an adult woman, and there was no going back. But the dream she had longed for had turned into a total, bitter nightmare as more and more of it came true. Because there was no happy ever after. Now here she was, about to attend the ball that people were calling the event of the decade. She would be expected to put on her public face, stand at Alexei's side, dance with him, smile—always smile!—and never let anyone see just how bruised and crushed her heart actually was.

Least of all Alexei himself.

Alexei, who had made it so plain that he desired her—in a physical sense at least. Who had acknowledged that he wanted her at his side, as his queen, his consort, but only in a dynastic marriage. She would be deceiving herself if she even allowed the hope of anything more to creep into her mind. Nothing had changed since the night she had gone to Alexei's room.

Well, yes, one thing had changed. And that was that she no longer lay awake, alone in her bed, in an agony of sexual hunger and frustration. She shared Alexei's room, Alexei's bed, every night and the passionate fire that had burned through them both that first time showed no signs of dimming. If anything, it had grown wilder, fiercer, stronger, with every night that passed. Though after that one heated coming together Alexei had always been meticulous, even dogmatic, about using the contraception they had both forgotten in the heat of the moment the first time.

But there was more to life than their searing sexual connection. There were the days to get through as well. The rest of the time it was business as usual, the demands of the throne taking so much time, so much energy. She woke every morning to find that the space beside her where Alexei had lain was cold and empty, revealing how he had been up so much earlier and how long he had been gone. Spending time with those 'new mistresses', the affairs of state that absorbed him so completely.

He had nothing else to offer her. No emotion, no caring, no...

Choking up inside on the last word, Ria swung away from the mirror, unable to meet her own eyes.

I can't love you. I loved once—adored her... Lost her.

No love. That was the word she was avoiding. The word she was running away from. The one that had no place in Alexei's life but that had taken over her existence completely.

The acid of unshed tears burned at the back of her eyes as she remembered that morning, when Alexei had been up early and dressing as usual while she still dozed. She had tried to lie still, not speaking a word, but in the end it had proved impossible. He had been heading towards the door when she had been unable to hold back any longer.

'When will you be back?'

She knew the words were a mistake as soon as she let them pass her lips, digging her teeth down painfully into her tongue as if she could hold them back. But too late. The stiffness of that long, straight spine, the set of his shoulders under the impeccably tailored steel-grey silk suit, told its own story without words.

'I have a full day.' It was flat, unemotional. 'But we will be together this evening. For the ball.'

Tonight the Black and White Ball would mark the culmination of all the ceremonial that led up to Alexei's accession to the throne. After tonight there would be the coronation itself.

And then their wedding.

On their wedding day he had said he would release her father. That move would mean that the balance of her mother's mind would be restored, possibly even her life would be saved when she had her husband back at her side. But wouldn't the dark hand of the past still reach out and touch the present, overshadowing it?

'Alexei. Are you sure you should release my father?'

He had started to move away again but that brought him up short, stilling totally.

'I thought that was what you wanted.'

'For my mother, yes. I'd give anything to see her happy and healthy again. And no matter what he is, she loves my father. But won't Gregor still be a threat? To Mecjoria. To you.'

To us, she wanted to add but it was a step too far.

'Why do you think I haven't let your father out already?'

When had he turned, swinging round to face her? She didn't think she had actually seen him move, but suddenly she was looking into his face, drawn into sculpted lines, hard and carved as a marble statue.

'Do you really think I would want him to have any more chances to bully you?'

Bully *her?* It was the last thing she had been expecting. She had thought that Alexei had left her father in prison out of revenge. That he had wanted to show he had control over the other man as Gregor had once had control over his future. She had never dreamed that he might actually be doing this to protect her.

'I'd like to see him try. I came to you because you are the king Mecjoria needs and everything I've seen just proves I was right in that. If he saw you now—saw how you've handled things—even my father would have to think again.'

'He'd have hated the walkabout.'

He was thinking of the events of the day before, when she and Alexei had opened a brand-new children's hospi-

tal here in the capital. The official part of the ceremony
had been over in less than an hour, but the crush of people
waiting to see them had shouted and called their names
until Alexei had totally discarded the protocol and planning that had set the timetable for the day and launched
into a spontaneous walkabout, shaking hands, talking,
smiling. She doubted if she had ever seen him smile so
much. He'd even…

A sudden memory of the day came back to haunt her.

A little boy had been pushed to the front of the crowd,
a slightly bent and dented bunch of flowers in his hand.
He'd tugged on Alexei's trousers, drawing the response
he'd needed. And Alexei had turned, crouching down beside him, his attention totally focussed on the one small
person. Totally at ease, he had lifted the child up, balanc-
ing him against his hip as he'd turned to face Ria.

'You have an admirer,' he'd said. 'And he wants to give
his flowers to the princess.'

'Not protocol…' Her voice broke the last word into two
disjointed syllables as she struggled with the memory.
'Not at all what I was trained for.' Her smile said how
little she cared. 'But it was the right thing for the day.'

'And the future.'

Alexei wished he could express just what that reception
had meant to him. Those smiling faces, the cheers, the
flowers, the hands thrust forward to take his, the women
wanting to press kisses on his cheek. His mouth had ached
with smiling, his fingers raw from clasping so many other
hands. So many times he had been told he was the image
of his father; so many people had said 'welcome back'.
If he turned or glanced out of the corner of his eyes, Ria
had been at his side as she had been so many times and
with her support he had actually felt free…

'It felt like coming home.'

'You are home. This is where you belong.'

But where did she belong? The question hit him like a blow in the face. She had been at his side but had that been from choice? What would she do if she was left free to follow her own destiny, without being trapped into linking it with his? The thought of how he had ensnared her, how he had manipulated her into his life, into his bed, was like the sting of a whip on his soul.

No—he hadn't manipulated her into his bed. She had come to him. When they had reached the palace he had tried to keep his distance from her, wanting to give her time to consider her position, but she had broken through the walls he had built around himself and just appeared at his door. Walking into his room as if she belonged there.

And that was how he wanted it. Wanted her warm and willing as she had been all night and every night since then. So much so that his body still pulsed at the memory, the burn of hunger not subdued even by the ache of appeasement.

But surely something that burned so white hot inevitably risked burning itself out? How long would this last and when it did end what did they have to put in its place? He had told himself that this was the only way to keep her safe. To marry her for now and then later—when it no longer mattered—he would let her go.

When it no longer mattered? How could it no longer matter? He had come alive, had lived in a new degree of intensity in the past weeks. How could something that felt this way ever fade into nothingness?

But would he ever be justified in keeping her here with him like this? He might call her father a bully but wasn't he trapping her into marriage just as much as Gregor had wanted to do? She had never wanted to be queen, just as he had never wanted to be king. Together they had built a way to take Mecjoria into a peaceful and prosperous future. But would that be enough to create their own futures?

If it wasn't then he'd have to set her free. But not yet. He couldn't let her go yet.

'We make a good team. But I'm not a monster—I won't force you to stay in this marriage for ever.'

The abrupt change of subject caught Ria unaware. One moment she had felt that they had moved to a new understanding, then this had come out of nowhere. Just as she had thought they had been celebrating a new beginning, it seemed that Alexei had already been thinking of the prospect of an end. She supposed she should have expected it. But the real horror was in the way he said it, as if he was offering her something worthwhile. Something that he believed she wanted.

'We could set a limit on the time it has to last,' Alexei stated flatly. 'Two years—three.'

Not a life sentence, then. She should feel relieved. Three weeks ago that was what she would have felt. It would have been a relief to her then to know that she hadn't signed her life away in this heartless marriage of convenience. But relief was not the emotion flooding through her now at the thought of a very limited future with this man. The terrible, tearing sense of loss threatened to rip her heart to pieces. She felt the blood drain down from her cheeks and she was sure that she must look as if she had seen a ghost. The ghost of her hopes and dreams. Dreams she had barely yet acknowledged to herself existed.

'I would give you a generous divorce settlement, of course.'

'Of course,' Ria echoed cynically. 'Once you have been king for a decent amount of time.'

'For which I will have you to thank.'

Again there was the sting of knowing that he meant it as a compliment. Because really he hadn't needed her in the end.

'You've won your own place in the hearts of the country. Surely you could see that yesterday?'

'Your help has been invaluable.' He was addressing her like he was at a public meeting. As if she was one of the ministers of state he had been spending so much time with of late. 'I knew you would make a perfect queen.'

'But only for a strictly limited time.' It was impossible to keep the bitterness from her voice. 'So perhaps we'd better really discuss the precise terms of this arrangement before we go any further? I'm to—what…?'

Sitting up in bed pulling the covers up around her because she felt too vulnerable otherwise, she checked off the points on the fingers of one hand.

'To be your fiancée, create the image of that fairy-tale romance, appear at your side in public, warm your bed in private. Marry you—provide you with an heir… No?'

His reaction had startled her. Shocked her. It was as if a sheet of ice had come down into the room, cutting them off from each other and freezing all the air in the room.

An heir. Of course she had known that was a touchy subject. But that had been when she had been concentrating on the future of Mecjoria. Now she had let herself think about his past, about the way he had fathered a child already, only to neglect the tiny girl who had died so tragically. He hadn't even tried to deny it when she had raised the accusation.

Why should I deny the facts when the world and his wife know what happened? And no one would believe a word that's different. The memory of the bitter words made her flinch inside, her stomach lurching nauseously.

An heir. Alexei felt as if someone had reached inside

his heart and ripped away the dressing he had thought he had slapped on there to protect it, revealing a wound that hadn't really healed but was still raw and vulnerable. A wound that he had been trying to ignore ever since that night that Ria had come to his room. The night that he had thoughtlessly made love to her without using a condom, breaking the number-one rule by which he'd lived his life since Belle had died.

And now this. Now with that one short word she had forced him to face what he had been pushing to the back of his mind, focussing his attention on the duties of being a king—the public duties—while ignoring the one private element that would always be there, needing to be considered for the future.

Ria had put her finger unerringly on it, dragged it out of the darkened corner to which he'd confined it, brought it kicking and screaming into the light—and it couldn't have come at a worse time.

He'd slept badly. Dark dreams had plagued his night. And it was with Ria's words that he had understood why. Yesterday had been a triumph. He knew there was no other word for it. But then there had been the small boy who had wanted his attention.

His heart kicked hard as he remembered the tug on his trousers, barely at calf level. He'd looked down into a pair of wide blue eyes, seen the curly fair hair, the gap-toothed grin. The impulse to pick the child up had been instant and spontaneous. The feel of that strong, compact little body in his arms had been nothing at all like the tiny, fragile speck of life that Belle had been but in a way that had been so much worse. It had hit home so hard with all the might-have-beens that he'd struggled with, forced him to look down into the dark chasm that he'd thought he'd put a lid on once and for all. The chasm he knew he was going to have to open up again someday or fail in his duty to Mecjoria.

Because how could he be a true king if he left the country without an heir for the future? That would mean that all this—that Ria's sacrifice—would be for nothing. The country needed an heir. Poor child with him as its father. But with Ria as its mother...

But how could he ever hope to follow through his resolution to let Ria go if he had made her pregnant?

'This will be a real marriage. In all possible ways. Of course.' It was flat and unemotional, the dangerous truth hidden behind blanked-off eyes. 'What else had you expected? That was what would have happened with Ivan. Wasn't it?'

Ria swallowed hard in an attempt to ease her painfully dry throat. Yes, it had been one of the conditions of the arranged marriage, how could it not have been? Which had been exactly why she had been so desperate to get out of that arrangement. To get away from the horror of being tied to a man she didn't love; to keep her freedom. Only, it seemed, to lose it all over again with the terms that Alexei was tossing out to her.

'And we do at least have huge chemistry between us. Come on Ria, admit it...' he added when he saw her eyes widen, heard the swift intake of breath she was unable to hold back. His eyes went to the other side of the bed in which she still lay, drawing attention to the crumpled pillows, the wildly disordered sheets. 'There is a real flame between us. You know, you've felt it.'

It was more than a flame. It was a raging inferno. She didn't need the state of the bed to remind her of how it was. Remembering last night and the way she had gone up in flames in his arms, the wildfire that his kisses had sent raging through her, she had to admit that there was

no way she could deny this. Her whole body still throbbed
with the aftermath of their shared passion and the heat
he had stirred in her blood through the night had burned
so hard that she almost imagined that the sheets would
scorch where she touched them.

His implication was that this would make it easier to
have that 'real marriage'. To create that much-needed heir.
It could have done just that. It should have; it really should.

She wanted Alexei so very much. Being with Alexei,
making love with him, was her dream come true. The
fantasy she had let herself indulge in in her teens, as she
fell in love with him with all the strength of her young,
foolish, naïve heart.

But that was also what made the thought of this so terrible. To have been tied into an arranged marriage with Ivan
would have been bad enough. But then only her body and
her mind would have been involved. Not like with Alexei.
With Alexei there was the risk to her heart—her soul.

Because she also knew, when she faced the truth, that
there was no way she was making love with Alex every
night. He was simply having sex, giving in to that flame
he had said burned between them. Throw a child—his
child—into the mix and she was done for. It would be lethal emotionally, totally destructive.

'It will be a real marriage—with everything that en-
tails. As king, it will be my duty to have an heir, so naturally...'

'Naturally...' Ria choked, earning herself a cold, flashing sideways look from those deep, dark eyes.

Any child they created together would be so much more
than that—at least to her. But that thought caught and
twisted her nerves at the prospect of exposing a child to
the toxic mix of hunger and distrust that their marriage
would be. The temporary marriage that he had insisted

was all it was going to be. It made her stomach clench in nausea, pushing bitter words from her uncontrolled mouth.

'Another child for you to neglect?'

She flung it at him, hard and sharp, her own bitterly divided feelings tightening her voice and putting into it more venom than she actually felt. The truth was that she didn't even know if she really felt that bitterness or not. She didn't even know what she should be feeling.

'Another child that might…'

She couldn't say the word. It might only have three letters in it, but 'die' had to be one of the most terrible words in the world.

'I would not neglect her.'

Alexei's eyes had turned translucent, like molten steel, and yet cold as frost in the same dark moment. Ria felt a terrible sense of wrong twist deep inside. There was something here that she didn't understand. Something she couldn't put her finger on and the danger in his expression, in his tone, warned her that she was somehow treading on very thin ice.

'This child would not be neglected,' he continued, each word snapped out, cold and brittle. 'It would be too important, too—'

He choked off the word, leaving her wondering just what he had been about to say. Too significant? Too essential to his plans for the future? His role as king?

'He or she would be cared for, treasured, watched over every moment of its days.'

'Because they would be the heir that you need so much.'

'Because I would have you to be its mother—to take care of it.'

How could something so quietly stated have the force of a deadly assault?

'So that is my future role as you see it? As a brood mare first, and then a nursemaid to your *heir.*'

Something new blazed in those molten eyes, colder and harder than she would have believed possible. She couldn't imagine what she had said to put it there. After all she had simply agreed with what he had declared he wanted from her, making it plain that they both knew where they stood.

'You don't value that role?' he demanded, low and harsh. 'You think Ivan would have offered you anything else?'

'I think that you and Ivan are two of a kind. That you would both use me—use anyone without a second thought—to get what you wanted. Well, don't worry—I'll do my duty.' She laced the word with venom and actually saw him wince away from her attack, his eyes hooded and hidden. 'After all, you've probably achieved all you ever wanted already.'

'Achieved what?' His dark brows snapped together in a hard line. 'What the hell are you talking about?'

'Well, we've made lo—had sex—what, a dozen times now? And you have been scrupulous about using contraceptives—each time but one! I could well be pregnant already with the heir you need. Another nine months and the baby will be born—you'll be crowned king, settled on the throne, and have everything you want. And I'll be free to leave.'

She tried to make it sound airy, careless, but the misery she felt only succeeded in making it seem cold and hard, ruinously so. Alexei obviously took her at her word.

'And you could do that, could you? You could leave your child? Hand it over to be brought up as a prince or princess, the heir to the throne?

He sounded harsh, brutally critical. How dared he?

How dared *he* imply that she would abandon her child when he had neglected his baby in that heartless way?

'No, I could never do that—but then you knew that already! You can guarantee that I will never leave, as long as I have a child to care for. That's how you know that you have me trapped so completely.'

She had never seen him look so, white, so totally bloodless, his skin drawn so tight across his cheekbones that she almost felt they might slice it wide open, leaving a gaping wound. His jaw clenched too, a muscle jerking hard against the control he was forcing over it, and for a moment she flinched inside, wondering just what he was going to come back at her with.

But no such retort ever came. Instead, after a moment seeming frozen into ice, Alexei was suddenly jerked into movement, as his phone on the side table buzzed in timed warning of an upcoming event.

'Duty calls,' he said curtly, and that was all.

A moment later he was gone, snatching up his phone on his way out the door. And when that slammed behind him she was left, stark naked and with only a sheet to cover her, unable to run after him for fear of encountering the ever-watchful Henri or someone else who had taken over today's particular shift.

Not that she had the emotional strength to even try. The war of words might have been physical blows for the effect they had had on her. She could only lie back and stare at the ceiling as the words replayed over in her head, burning tears rolling down her cheeks to soak into the pillow behind her head.

CHAPTER TWELVE

FINDING THAT SHE was still staring blankly at her reflection in the mirror, not having moved for who knew how long, Ria blinked hard, trying to clear her thoughts and failing completely. The truth was that she was emotionally involved in this relationship and so she would be emotionally committed to the marriage. And that was why it would hurt so badly to be confined to the sidelines of Alexei's life. She could be his temporary queen of convenience, his bed mate, the mother of his child, but in his heart she would be nothing.

Ria's hand went to the sparkling diamond necklace that encircled her throat, fingering the brilliant gems as she recalled the way that the ornate jewels and the matching earrings had been delivered to her room earlier that evening.

Wear these for me tonight, the note that accompanied them had said in Alexei's firm, slashing handwriting.

Ria's fingers tightened on the necklace so convulsively that the delicate design was in danger of snapping under her grip. Alexei certainly no longer needed help with his position as king. He was issuing orders left, right and centre. She was strongly tempted to take the damn thing off and...

You don't like presents? Alexei's words came back to her, stilling the impulsive gesture. Remembering them from this distance, she couldn't be sure whether she had really heard the trace of—of what? Defensiveness? Uncertainty?—she had thought she had caught behind the mockery the first time. *I thought women liked flowers—and jewellery.*

Well, not this woman! Ria told him in the privacy of her thoughts. Not when she wanted so much more.

But going down that path was a weakness she couldn't afford. It came too close to dreams she could never have. It even, damn it, brought tears to burn at the back of her eyes. Fiercely she blinked them away, knowing she didn't have time to do any repair job on the make-up that a beautician had applied not an hour before. She would have to hope that the ornate silk mask, edged with sparkling crystals and pearls, would conceal the truth of the way she was feeling.

Swinging away from the mirror, Ria paced restlessly about the room, struggling to control her raw and unsettled breathing. She stumbled for a moment awkwardly when her toe caught on something on the floor, almost tripping her up. Glancing down, she saw that what she had trodden on. A man's wallet. Elderly, its worn brown leather partly hidden under a chair, it looked out of place in the elegant cream and gold room.

It must be Alexei's, she realised, recalling how he had visited her here the day before, his tie tugged loose, his shirt sleeves rolled up, his jacket off and slung over his shoulder as soon as he had escaped from his formal duties of the day. He had tossed the jacket on to the chair as he had gathered her to him and kissed her hard and, as always happened, his touch had ignited the flames between them so that in the space of a couple of heartbeats they had fallen on to the bed, oblivious to everything else. The wallet must have slipped from his pocket then.

Picking it up, she couldn't resist the impulse to flick it open, examine the contents. There was nothing unexpected in there—some credit cards, a few banknotes—but then one thing caught her attention, the corner of a photograph tucked into the back section. Curiosity stinging at her, she pulled it out carefully and felt the room swing wildly round her as she took in what it was.

A small print of a photograph. A tiny baby, barely a few weeks old, with dark, dark eyes and a wild fuzz of black hair on her small head. There was only one person it could be. Sweet little Isabelle, Alexei's baby daughter. The child who had been born as a result of such scandal and disgrace and who had only lived for a few short weeks, dying alone and neglected by her drunken father.

But that was where something caught on a raw exposed corner of Ria's nerves, making her heart jerk hard and sharp in reaction, and she had to close her eyes against the sensation. But when she opened them again, the photo in her hand was still there. Still clutched between her fingers.

Still telling the same story.

She had seen enough of Alexei's photographs in the magazines or the press, in his offices and again in his home. She knew the stylised, stark style he favoured, the careful framing, the deliberate focus. And this photograph had none of those. It was a quick, candid snap, snatched in a moment of spontaneity to capture the first flicker of a smile on the tiny girl's face. He had grabbed for his camera, and as a result he had captured something so truly special.

Not just an image of his little girl's first smile. But also a picture of his daughter snapped, with love, by her doting daddy.

Memory rushed over her like a thick black wave. The memory of a small boy held in strong male arms, totally

secure, totally confident, a wilting bunch of flowers in
one rather grubby hand, the fingers of the other tangling
and twisting in Alexei's hair. The image of Alexei's face
that morning when she had accused him of neglecting his
baby. Even worse, there was the echo of those terrible,
harsh words on that day in London.

*Why should I deny the facts when the world and his
wife know what happened? And no one would believe a
word that's different.*

How differently she heard those words now, catching
the burn of bitterness, something close to despair that, focussed only on her own needs and plans, she had failed
to notice that first time. And, knowing that, her stomach
quailed and tied itself into knots at the thought of having
to face Alexei again tonight.

'Ria…'

As if called up by her thoughts, there was a knock at
the door. Alexei? What was he doing here?

He was standing on the landing so tall and elegant in
the beautifully tailored evening clothes, the immaculate
white shirt, the plain black silk mask across the upper part
of his face, polished jet eyes gleaming through the slits
in the fine material. This was Alexei the king, no longer
her childhood friend but a man grown to full adulthood
and ready to accept his destiny. He was the ruler Mecjoria needed, strong, powerful and in control. And he was
her lover. Heat pooled low in her body at just the thought.
Ria actually felt her legs weaken, her hand going out to
his for support.

'You look wonderful.'

Alexei's dark gaze slid over her body, taking in every
inch of the dress that the designer had created for her. The
white silk clung to the curves of her breasts and hips in a
way that dried his throat in sexual need, leaving him hot

and hard in the space between one heartbeat and the next.
He could never get enough of this woman, and the carnal
thoughts she inspired had turned his brain molten, had
tormented him through the day so that he barely had the
strength to focus on what he was doing. The white mask
gave her an other-worldly appearance, like a character at
a Venetian carnival, with its ornate design, the eye pieces
edged with pearls and sparkling crystals, drawing attention to the mossy green of her eyes fringed by impossibly
thick and long dark lashes.

'You don't scrub up so badly yourself. Madame Herone would be proud of you.'

Was that a trace of uncertain laughter in her voice? The
eyes that met his looked unusually, almost suspiciously
bright. Her hand, impossibly delicate where it was enclosed in his, held on rather too tight.

The strapless design of her dress exposed the long,
beautiful line of her throat, the creamy curve of her shoulders. Only hours ago, in the growing light of dawn, he had
kissed his way down that smooth skin, lingering at the
point where her pulse now beat at the base of her neck,
before moving lower, to the delicious temptation of her
breasts. He could almost still taste her rose-tinted nipples
against his tongue and his lower body was so hard and
tight that it was painful.

This was the way he had felt all week. He had resented
the official duties, the diplomatic meetings and govern-
mental debates that had taken so much time away from
what he really wanted, from this woman who possessed
his body, obsessed his mind. When he was with her he
could think of nothing else. And when he was away from
her all he could think about was getting back to her and
being alone with her, of burying himself in the glorious
temptation of her body. He knew she felt that way too—

the long hot nights they had spent together had made it plain that she wanted him every bit as much as he lusted after her. She had been as hungry as he had been, taking every kiss, every caress he offered, opening herself to him and welcoming him into her body as often as he could wish—reaching for him in the middle of the night to encourage him into even more sensual possession when he had thought that she was exhausted and could take no more.

But he couldn't think that way any more. He couldn't let himself think at all or he would back out of this right now. He had done all the thinking he needed to do and, with the memory of the scene in his bedroom that morning, had come to his decision. The only decision he believed was possible. He couldn't live with himself if he went any other way.

And now he had to tell Ria what was going to happen.

'We need to talk.'

Could there be any more ominous line in the whole of the English language? Ria questioned as she made herself step backwards to let him into the room.

'But we said we would meet downstairs, in one of the anterooms, ready to go into the ballroom together.'

'I know we did—but this has to be sorted out before we go down. Before anything else.'

Which was guaranteed to make her throat clench tighter, her lungs constrict, making it hard to breathe. Unthinkingly she lifted her hand to wave some air into her face, remembering only what she held when she saw Alexei's eyes focus sharply on the photograph.

'Belle...'

If she had any doubts left then they evaporated in the

burn of his expression, the shadows of pain that darkened his voice. Ria took a slow deep breath. She owed him this.

'The stories they told about that—you didn't do it. You couldn't have done it.'

He'd dropped her hand, reached out and took the small snapshot, holding it carefully as if afraid it might disintegrate.

'Cot death, they called it. But if someone had been there…'

'But wasn't Mariette?'

'Oh, she was there but she wasn't any help to anyone. Mariette had problems. Depression—drink—drugs.' His voice was low and flat, all emotion ironed out. 'We'd had a savage row. She told me to get out. I planned on getting drunk but I couldn't get rid of the fear that there was something wrong. I had to go back—but Mariette's door was locked against me and she wouldn't answer no matter how much I knocked and shouted. Eventually I had to break the door down—and found a scene of horror inside. Mariette was in a drug-fuelled stupor and Belle had died in her cradle.' His breath caught hard in his throat and he had to force the words out.

Ria hadn't been aware of moving forward, coming closer, but now she realised that she was so very close to him and, reaching out, she took his hand again, but the other way round this time, feeling his fingers curl around hers, hold her tightly.

'But everyone thought— You took the blame.' Incredulity made her voice shake.

Alexei's shrug was weary, dismissive.

'Because you loved her?'

'No, not Mariette.' He was shaking his head before her words were out. 'We'd run our course long before, but we stayed together for the baby's sake.'

Reaching up, he pulled the mask away from his face and let it drop, the lines around his nose and eyes seeming to be more dramatically etched as they were exposed to the light.

'My shoulders are broad enough. And Mariette had demons of her own to fight. She never wanted to be pregnant, and when she found she was she wanted to have an abortion. I persuaded her not to. She hated every minute of it, and I think she suffered from post-natal depression after Belle arrived. She ended up having a complete breakdown and had to be hospitalised. The last thing she needed was a horde of paparazzi hounding her, accusing her...'

For a moment he paused, his head going back, dark eyes looking deep into hers.

'She'd already cracked completely and lashed out when I tried to see her.'

His twisted smile tore at her heart. Could it get any worse? In her mind's eye, Ria was seeing the notorious photo of Alexei, bruised and bloodied. She had assumed—everyone had assumed—that he had been in a fight. But now she could see that those scratches had been scored into his skin by long, feminine nails.

'And I had plenty of my own scandals to live down. But...' His eyes went to the photo in his hand. 'I adored that little girl.'

'I know you did.'

'You believe me?'

Ria nodded mutely, tears clogging her throat. 'You're not capable of anything like they accused you of.'

Just for a moment Alexei rested his forehead against hers and closed his eyes.

'Thank you.'

I can't love you. I loved once—adored her... Lost her.

And it was little Belle, the baby daughter, who had

stolen his heart. If she hadn't seen that photograph she would know it now from the rawness in his voice, the darkness of his eyes. Oh dear heaven, if only she could ever hope to see that look when he thought of her. But he had confided the truth to her. Would she be totally blind, totally foolish to allow herself to hope that that meant he felt more for her than just his convenient, dynastic bride-to-be? Ria couldn't suppress the wild, skittering jump of her heart at the thought.

Downstairs, in the main hall of the castle, the huge golden gong sounded to announce the fact that it was almost time for the ball to start. Another few minutes and they would be expected to go down, ready to make their ceremonial entry. As always, the demands of state were intruding into their private moments. Obviously Alexei thought so too because he lifted his head, raked both his hands through the crisp darkness of his hair.

'You said we needed to talk.' She didn't know if she wanted to push him into saying whatever he had come to tell her. Only that right now she couldn't bear to leave it hanging unsaid for a moment longer.

'We do.'

He had always known that this was going to be hard and the conversation they had just had, the trust she had honoured him with, would only make things so much worse. But he also knew that it was the only way he could do things. The way she was looking at him, eyes bright behind that white satin mask, was going to destroy him if he didn't get things out in the open—fast.

But if ever there was a time that he owed someone the truth then it was now.

'This isn't going to work.'

He could see her recoil, eyes closing, the hand she had put on his snatched away abruptly.

'What isn't working?'

'Everything. The engagement—the marriage—you as my queen. Everything.'

'But I don't understand.' He was giving her what he knew she wanted but she wasn't making things easy for him. 'We've already announced the engagement. Tonight…'

'I know. Tonight we are supposed to face the court, the nobility and every last one of the foreign diplomats in the country. Tonight is to mark the first step on to the final public stage of this whole damn king business.'

Tonight they would face the world as a royal couple—the future of the country. The potential royal family. And that was where one great big problem lay. A problem that had grown deeper and darker since this morning. Could he and this woman, this gorgeous, sexy woman, ever be more than the passionate lovers they had been in the past weeks? Could they ever become a *family?*

Family. That was the word that showed him what he wanted most and why he could not ever allow himself to think of letting this continue.

He had always wanted a family. The family he'd hoped to find when they had first come to Mecjoria. The one that had been denied him when his father had died and all that had followed. That was why he had begged Mariette not to have the abortion she'd wanted. Why he'd fallen in love with his little daughter from the moment the doctors had first put her in his arms just after the birth. Memories of Belle and all that he'd lost with her were like a dark bruise on his thoughts. The accusations Ria had flung at him this morning had brought those terrible memories rushing back, so that he hadn't been able to stay and face them down. And even now, when he knew she understood—more so *because* she'd understood—he knew he couldn't keep her trapped with him, not like this. She deserved so much better.

The accusation of trapping her that she'd flung at him was so appallingly justified, and the thought stuck in his throat, made acid burn in his stomach. He'd pushed her into a situation that took all her options, any trace of choice away from her. What made him think that she would want marriage to him any more than she would want to become Ivan's bride? It was true that the country benefited from the arranged marriage but, hell and damnation, he could have handled it so much better.

Did he really want a bride who looked so tense whenever they were alone—unless they were in bed together? A queen who held herself so stiffly that she looked as if she might break into a thousand brittle pieces if he touched her? A woman who, like his own mother, had been used as just a pawn in the power games of court? He had forced Mariette into a situation that she didn't want, and the end result had been a total tragedy. He could not do that to Ria.

'Tell me one thing.' He had to hear it from her own lips. 'Would you have agreed to marry me if I hadn't made it a condition of my accepting the throne?'

'I…' She swallowed down the rest of her answer but he didn't need it. Her hesitation, the way her eyes dodged away from his, told their own story. If he followed this path any longer he was no better—in fact, worse—than her father. He would be using her for his own ends, keeping her a prisoner when she wanted so desperately to fly free.

'I can't ask this of you.'

'You didn't ask,' Ria flung at him. 'You commanded.'

Was that weak, shaken voice really her own? Once again she had retreated behind false flippancy to disguise the way she was really feeling. The way that her life, the future she had thought was hers, had crumbled around her, the dreams she had just allowed herself to let into her mind evaporating in the blink of an eye. But she had let them linger for a moment and the bite of loss was all the more agonising because of that.

Reject that! Please. Argue with me, she begged him in her thoughts. But Alexei was nodding his head, taking her word as truth.

'And you had no choice but to agree. Well, I'm giving you that choice now. I never should have asked you to marry me. I don't need you to validate my position as king. The engagement is off—it should never have happened. You're free to go.'

'Free...'

The room swung round her violently, her eyes blurring, her breath escaping in a wild, shaken gasp. If this was freedom then she wanted none of it.

'Tonight? Right here and now?'

How did he manage to make the most appalling things sound as if he was giving her exactly what she wanted? Their eyes came together, burnished black clashing with clouded jade, and the ruthless conviction in his totally defeated her. She was dismissed, discarded, just like that.

'But what about...?'

In the hallway the gong sounded once again, summoning them. The sound made Alexei shake his head, his eyes closing briefly.

'How could I have been so bloody stupid?' He groaned. 'I'm sorry, Ria. I had meant to talk to you after the ball, but...' His eyes dropped to the photograph of Belle he still held in his hand. 'Things knocked me off-balance. Now everyone is here.'

'Why?'

It was the one thing she could hold on to. The one thing

that had registered in the storm of misery that assailed her. Alexei had decided that he didn't need to marry her—that he didn't want to marry her. *He didn't want her.* And there was no way she could fight back against that.

'Sorry for what?' Somehow she forced herself to ask it. 'Why did you plan to tell me *after* the ball?'

His expression was almost gentle and if it hadn't been for the bleakness of his eyes she might almost have believed that he was the Alexei of ten years before. The Alexei she had first fallen in love with.

'Because it was your dream,' he stated flatly. 'You always wanted to attend the Black and White Ball.' Just for a second, shockingly, the corner of his mouth quirked up into something that was almost a smile. 'You even trained for long hours with Madam Herone just for it. I wanted this to be for you.'

'But the engagement?' She didn't know how she had found the strength to speak. She wasn't even sure how she was managing to stay upright, except that she couldn't give in. She couldn't just collapse into the pathetic, despondent little heap that she felt she had become since he had declared he no longer wanted to marry her.

'After the ball, we would announce that you had changed your mind about marrying me.'

That she had changed her mind. He had thought of everything. But at least he would have left her with some pride by making it seem that she was the one who had ended their relationship. Not that she had been jilted, as she had just been. And for years he had remembered how much she had wanted to go to the ball, and had planned to give her that at least.

It wasn't much, not compared with the lifetime, the love, she had dreamed of. But it was all she was going to get. And, weak and foolish as she was, she knew in her heart that she was going to reach for it. For one last evening with Alexei. For one last night, this Cinderella was going to the ball with the man she loved.

Drawing on every ounce of her strength, she straightened her spine.

'You've obviously thought it all through. We'll do that, then.' She hoped she sounded calm, convincing. If he was giving her her freedom, then she could give him his. She wouldn't beg or cling. If her father had ever taught her anything worthwhile then it was dignity, even in defeat.

Below them they heard the third and final sound of the gong that preceded their arrival in the ballroom. It was now or never.

'Let's go.'

The journey down the wide, sweeping stairs seemed to take a lifetime. Alexei had offered her his arm for support and she managed to force herself to take it, knowing that the stinging film of tears she would not allow herself to shed blurred her vision and made her steps uncertain without his support. And if just having this one last chance to touch him, to hold on to his strength, was a personal indulgence, then that was her private business. An indulgence that she was never going to admit to anyone but keep hidden in the secrecy of her thoughts, stored up against the time when this was no longer possible and memories of how it had felt to be so close to him, to look into his beloved face, were all she had left.

At the bottom of the staircase the Lord Chamberlain was waiting, saying nothing, but the look of carefully controlled concern on his face told them that the world of ceremony and court appearances had already been delayed for long enough.

'Sir...'

Alexei's hand came up, commanding silence.

'I know. We're coming.'

Reaching out, he took Ria's fingers again, folding his own around them as he nodded his head in the direction of the huge doors to the ballroom. The glittering chandeliers and gold-decorated walls were hidden behind the huge double doors, but the buzz of a thousand conversations, the sound of so many feet moving on the polished floor, gave away the fact that their arrival was expected and waited for with huge anticipation.

'Duty calls. Are you sure you want to go through with this?' he murmured.

'Do we have any choice? Right now Mecjoria is what matters,' she managed to assure him, keeping her head high, her eyes now wide and dry.

'Then let's do this.'

They took a step forward, another. Two footmen stepped forward to take hold of the large metal handles, one on each side of the door.

And then, totally unexpectedly, Alexei stopped, looked straight into her face.

'You really are a queen,' he told her, low, husky and intent.

It was meant as a compliment, she knew, and her smile in reply was slow and tinged with the regret that was eating her alive.

'Just not your queen,' she managed, wishing that it was not the truth and knowing that all the wishing in the world would never ease away the agony of loss that was tearing her up inside.

As she spoke the big doors swung open and the buzz of talk and noise rose to a crescendo of excitement. Alexei took her hand in his as they walked forward into the ballroom, putting on the act of the fairy-tale couple for one last time.

CHAPTER THIRTEEN

UNDER ANY OTHER circumstances, it would have been a magical night.

Everything that Ria had ever imagined or dreamed about the Black and White Ball had come true, and most of it had been beyond her wildest imaginings. The huge ballroom was beautifully decorated, the lights from a dozen brilliant crystal chandeliers sparkling over the array of elegant men and women, all dressed, as the convention for the night demanded, in the most stylish variations on the purely monochrome theme of dress. They might be confined to black and white but the fabulous couture gowns, the brilliant jewels and, most of all, the stunningly decorated masks meant that everyone looked so different, so amazing, creating a stunning image in the room as a whole. One that was reflected over and over in the huge mirrored walls.

There was food and wine, glorious, delicious food for all she knew. But none of it passed her lips, and she barely drank a thing. She was strung tight as a wire on the atmosphere, the sensations of actually being here, like this. With Alexei. But at the same time those sensations were sharpened devastatingly by the terrible undercurrent of powerful emotion, the icy burn of pain that came from knowing that the man beside her was the love of her life, her reason for breathing, but that when this night was over he was expecting her to go, walk out of his life for ever.

From the moment they had walked into the room, and paused at the top of the short flight of steps that lead down the highly polished floor, all eyes had been on them. Just their appearance had triggered off a blinding fusillade of camera flashes that made her head spin and had her clutching at Alexei's arm for support. For long minutes afterwards she was still blinking to clear away the spots in her vision and bring her gaze back into focus properly. And he was there, at her side, silently supporting her, seeming to know instinctively just when she was able to see again clearly, when she could stand on her own two feet and turn her attention to the crowds of statesmen, dignitaries and nobility who thronged the room.

That was when Alexei carefully eased his way away from her side, resting his hand on hers just once as he turned her towards another group of guests. A faint inclination of his head, the touch of his hand at the base of her spine, spoke volumes without words. For this one night, still his fiancée, officially soon to be his queen, she should mix with their guests, socialise, talk with them. And he knew she could do it. Knew he didn't have to stay with her. Instead he headed off in the opposite direction, working the room. And the bittersweet rush of pride at the thought that he knew she wouldn't let him down helped Ria's feet move, warmed her smile when all the time she was feeling broken and dead inside.

She had no idea how much time had passed when they met up again. Only that he came to find her just at the point she had started to flag. When her mouth was beginning to ache with smiling, when her fund of small talk was beginning to dry up. Just when she felt she'd had enough, suddenly he was there by her side.

'Dance with me,' he said softly, and she turned to him, feeling as she gave him her hand and he lead her out on to the dance floor that, for her, the evening had really just truly begun.

With his arms round her, warm and strong, his strength supporting her, the scent of his skin in her nostrils, she barely felt as if her feet were on the ground any longer. She was all talked out, unable to find any words to say to him. But Alexei didn't appear to need conversation; seemed instead, like her, to be content to remain in their own silent bubble.

She had wanted to be here so much. Had dreamed of being here in so many ways—at the Black and White Ball, at the start of a new reign for the country, with the succession secured, with Mecjoria safe. With Ivan kept from the throne and Alexei, a strong, honest, powerful ruler, in his place. Here with the man she loved.

And that was when her thoughts stumbled to a halt. Where her mind seemed to blow a fuse and she could go no further, could not get past the thought of how much she loved this man. How much she wanted to be in his arms, and stay there for ever. At this moment she felt that she wouldn't even ask for his love in return. Just to stay with him, love him would be enough.

But already the clock was ticking towards the end of the convenient engagement Alexei had decided he no longer needed. Like Cinderella, she had until midnight before all the magic in her life disappeared and she found she was once more back in reality, all her dreams shattered around her. Already, an hour or more of the last remaining precious time she had with Alexei had passed and try as she might she couldn't hold back a single minute of the little that was left.

'Enjoying yourself?'

Alexei asked the question strangely stiffly, his breath warm against her ear, her cheek pressed close to his. She could only nod silently in answer, not daring to look up into his face, meet his eyes through the black silk mask. It would destroy her if she did. She would shatter into tiny pieces right here on the polished floor.

Enjoying yourself! Alexei couldn't believe he had been stupid enough to ask the inane question. The same one that he had asked a dozen, a hundred, times already that evening. It was the sort of polite, formal small talk that he used to put people at their ease, to make them feel that he had noticed them, that he appreciated the fact that they were there. It was for the Mecjorian nobility, the foreign dignitaries, the press even.

It was not for Ria. Not for this woman who he now held in his arms for perhaps the last time and who, at the end of this evening, would walk out of his life and into her own future—totally free for the first time ever.

Because how could he not notice Ria when she looked so stunningly beautiful, when she was all his private sensual fantasies come at once? How could he not appreciate what she was, who she was, when she had been there with him, always at his side, always offering her support through the long weeks since she had come to him with the news that he was king? Because it was right.

That was why he had known tonight that he had only one way forward. That, like Ria, he had to do what was right. Right for her, even if everything that was in him ached in protest at the thought. He had forced her into the marriage that he had believed would bring him the satisfaction he craved. It had brought him all that satisfaction—and more. So much more. But to keep her in such a marriage would be like chaining up some beautiful, exotic wild creature.

She would die in captivity. And he couldn't bear to see that happen to her. So tonight he was setting her free.

But first he would have just a few more hours to dance with her, hold her, maybe even kiss her. In spite of himself, he let his arms tighten round her, drew her soft warmth closer, inhaled the perfume of her skin against his. The bittersweet delight of it made his body burn in a hunger that he knew would have him lying awake through the night, and many more long, empty nights when this was done. He had until midnight. A few more hours to pretend that she was still his.

His! The lie cut terribly deep. The truth was that Ria had never been his. And that was why tonight had been inevitable, right from the start. But everything that was in him rebelled at the thought.

He couldn't do it. He couldn't let her go.

Ria was so lost in her thoughts, in the deep sensual awareness of being held so close to Alexei that at first the flurry of interest was just like a blur at the edge of her consciousness. She heard the buzz of sound as if it was that of a swarm of bees somewhere far distant, on the horizon but coming closer, growing louder, with every second.

Uncharacteristically, Alexei's smooth steps in the waltz stumbled slightly, hesitated, slowed. She heard him mutter a low toned, dark, fierce curse, the furious, 'Too early. Too damn early,' and suddenly the whole dance was stuttering to a halt as the murmur around them grew, as if that swarm of bees was coming closer, dangerously so.

'Escalona…'

On a sense of shock she heard her own name muttered over and over again. But once or twice it came with an addition that startled her, shocked her into stillness, bringing her head up and round.

'It's Gregor Escalona. And his wife.'

Beside her Alexei had stilled, his powerful body freezing in shock and rejection. She could almost feel the pulse of anger along the length of his frame. It was there in the tightening of the hand that held hers, the extra pressure of the one now clamped against her spine, the delicate dancer's hold replaced by something that felt disturbingly like imprisonment, a fierce control that shocked and upset her.

'Alexei…' she began, her use of his name clashing with the way he said hers.

'Ria…'

It shocked her because it sounded so rough, so ominous it made her heart thump nervously. Instinctively she wrenched herself out of his constraining hold, swivelling round against the pressure of his hands. Her vision blurring in disbelief, she could only stand and stare as she tried to take in the impossible reality of what she saw.

'*Mum!* And—and—'

And her father.

Her father who had just made his way into the room and was now standing at the top of the steps, her mother beside him. He looked paler, thinner, diminished somehow, though nothing like as pale and wan as Elizabetta who was holding onto his arm for grim death, and seeming dangerously close to collapsing in a heap on the floor if she loosened her grip. It couldn't be real; it was impossible. Her father was still locked away in the state prison, his freedom dependent on her marriage to Alexei…

But there wasn't going to be a marriage any more.

'Ria.'

Alexei's hands were on her shoulders, straining to turn her round, working against the instinctive resistance she put up. She couldn't believe what was happening. Why this was happening? Why they were there?

'Ria, look at me!'

One hand had come up in a slashing gesture to silence the orchestra and the whole room was suddenly still and frozen. In the quiet, the note of command was enough to take the strength from her. Her shoulders slumped and she found herself swung back again to face him, trapped in the sudden circles of isolation that had formed round them as every one of the other dancers froze, silently watching.

She had only a moment to look up into his dark, shuttered face, see the glare of fury he directed at her father, before he moved again suddenly, stunning her by going down on one knee right there in front of her. In front of the whole crowded ballroom.

Alexei—don't. She tried to open her mouth to say the words but nothing would come out. She knew just what was coming and she couldn't bear it. Couldn't cope with this. Not now; not like this.

Please, not like this...

She wanted to run but Alexei's grip tightened around it, holding her still. But what held her stiller was the deep, dark gaze that clashed with hers from behind the black silk mask.

'Ria, I didn't do this right last time. I want to do it properly now. I want your family—all the country—to know that I want you to be my queen. I don't want to be king without you at my side.'

'No...' She tried again but her voice was only a thin thread of sound, buried under the buzz of curiosity, the murmurs of incredulity and interest that came from their audience who were clearly hanging on to every word.

'Ria—will you marry me?'

Was the room really swinging round her, lurching nauseously, or was that just the rush of shock and panic to her head? She could see that her parents had been prevented from moving forward, the security guard putting a restraining hand on her father's arm, her mother stopping at his side though her eyes were fixed on her daughter's face. She saw the stunned, astonished, the frankly curious expressions on the faces of those around them, expressions that even the concealing masks could not disguise. And there, at her feet, was Alexei…

Alexei, the man she loved and whose proposal she would have so loved to hear—if only he had meant it. But not like this! Only this evening he had told her that he didn't want to marry her, that he was breaking off their engagement, that it was over. So this…

So this could only be some cold-blooded political statement. A statement of power in front of every dignitary, every statesman at the ball.

The conditions were that I would free your father when you became my wife. Call it a wedding day gift from me.

Oh, why did she have to remember that? But it had to be what was behind it—the need to show the world, the court and her father, that Alexei was the one with the power. That he was totally in control.

Here she was, with the whole court hanging on her every word, with her parents looking on. The freedom—temporary, surely—her father was enjoying hit home to her how easily Alexei could change everything, order everything with a flick of his head just as he had silenced the orchestra just moments before.

He had presented her with an ultimatum. Accept his proposal, here in the most public place possible, or everything he held over her would fall into place in the most appalling way.

She had thought that she couldn't face a future without him in it. But how could she ever have a future with a man who would force her hand in this way? Who would go to these lengths to emphasise the power he had over her?

'I can't!' she gasped, tasting the salt of her own tears sliding into her mouth as she flung the words into the silence, not daring to look into Alexei's face to see the effect they had as they landed. 'I won't marry you! And you can't make me!'

CHAPTER FOURTEEN

I won't marry you!

The words seared through Alexei's thoughts, burning an agonising trail behind them.

I won't marry you! And you can't make me!

'Make you?'

Alexei got slowly to his feet, his eyes still fixed on her indignant face, the way that her proud head was held so high, the green eyes flashing wild defiance into his. The stunned silence around him reflected his own shock and confusion, taking it and multiplying it inside his head.

He had been so sure. So convinced that at last he was on the right track with Ria. He knew he had pushed too hard, forced her into the position as his fiancée because he wanted her so much. And as a result she had felt bullied, trapped.

So he had come up with what had seemed like the perfect plan. To let her go, set her free. He had even arranged for her father to be liberated as a symbol of everything he wanted for her. But at the last minute he had known he couldn't go through with it. And something about her tonight, a new delicacy, a touch of melancholy, had given him a foolish, wild hope. He had known that he had to try.

He'd hoped a fresh proposal—one at the event that she had always longed to attend—might have some magic in

it. But, if the truth were told, it had had the exact opposite effect of the one he had been looking for.

She had frozen, all colour leaching from her face, staring at him as if he had suddenly turned into a hissing,
spitting poisonous snake right before her eyes.

'How the hell…?' he began but she shook her head
wildly, loosening the elegant hair style so that locks of
it tumbled down around her face. He could see how her
eyes shone, the quiver of her lips that seemed to speak
of some powerful emotion only just held in check, but
every inch of her slender body was tight with defiance—
and rejection.

'You may be king,' she declared, focussing on him so
tightly that it seemed as if there was no one in the room
but the two of them. 'And perhaps you can order people
around—order their lives around for the fun of it! But you
can't control people's hearts. You can't dictate the way I
think—the way I feel! You can't force me to—'

But that was too much to take.

'Force? What force have I used?'

But she wasn't listening, launched on her stream of
thoughts, flinging her fury into his face without a hint of
restraint or hesitation.

'You might be able to command that I do as you say
and I will have to obey you with a "yes, Your Royal High-
ness. Anything you say, Your Majesty".'

Her elegant frame dipped in the most flawless—and
most sarcastic—curtsey ever delivered. That was, unless
you remembered the one she had given him on the night
she had come to his room, when the blue silk nightgown
had billowed out at her feet, forming a perfect pool of
silk on the floor around her. Alexei's groin tightened at
the memory of where that had led but he had to fight the
impulse, knowing that it would distract him too much.

And he didn't need any distractions, not if he was to work out just where everything had gone wrong—and think of some way to put it right.

'You can even make me marry you—but you can't command my heart. You can't force me to love you!'

Love.

Things might have moved rather faster than he had intended, the careful plan he'd decided on rushed and confused at the last moment, but he could swear that he had never said anything about… Why would she mention love? Why would it even be in her thoughts unless…?

'Who the hell said anything about love?'

Her only response was a swift, startled widening of her eyes, the sudden sharp biting down of her teeth onto the softness of her bottom lip in a way that made him wince in instinctive sympathy.

They couldn't talk like this, not with every ear in the place tuned to what they were saying, hanging on to every word. For a second he considered grabbing hold of Ria's hand, taking her out of here—on to the terrace, into the garden—but one glance into her face had him reconsidering. She would fight him all the way, he knew that, and they had already created enough of a fever of interest to be the talk of the country for several years or more.

'Everyone out of here.' His hand came up to brush off the murmurs of concern. 'Now.'

He might get used to this king business after all, Alexei reflected as everyone obeyed his order, moving out of the room at his command. Even though they all hurried to obey him, it still took far longer than he had anticipated to empty the room and shut the doors behind them. It seemed an age before he was alone with Ria, and she was itching to get out of here; he could see that in her eyes, in the uneasy way she moved from one foot to another, nervous as a restive horse.

But she had stayed, and he had to pin his hopes on that.

What the devil was he going to say that didn't make her throw up her head and run? There was only one place to start. One word that was fixed inside his head, immovable and clear.

'Love?' he said, still unable to believe that he had heard her right. 'Did you say love?'

Had she? Oh dear heaven had she actually made the biggest mistake ever and come out with it just like that—in front of everyone here? Ria could feel the colour flood up into her face, sweeping under her mask, and then swiftly ebb away again as she heard her own voice sounding inside her head.

'You can't make me love you!' She flashed it at him in desperate defiance, fearful that he might take advantage of it, use it against her.

But somehow he didn't look quite how she expected. There was none of the anger, none of the coldness of rejection, nothing of the withdrawal she had thought she would see in his face if she ever admitted to the way she was feeling.

'I wouldn't even try,' he said and his voice was strangely low, almost soft. 'You're right, love can't be forced. It can only be given.'

Was she supposed to find an answer to that? She tried, she really did, but nothing came to mind. Her brain was just great, big empty space, with no thoughts forming anywhere.

'But you did try to force it.'

'Is that what you thought I was doing?'

He raked both hands through his hair, pushing it into appealing disorder. The movement knocked the mask sideways slightly. And, as he had done earlier in her room, he snatched it off and tossed it to the ground.

'I thought I was proposing. Let's face it, I never really *asked* you to marry me—we just agreed on terms.'

We didn't exactly agree, Ria was about to say, but something caught on her tongue, stopping her from getting the words out. She was looking again at that shockingly unexpected proposal. The sudden silence, the gaping crowds, and Alexei on his knee before her.

The man who had been so convinced that Mecjoria wouldn't want him, that the nobility would reject him as they had once done ten years before, had taken the risk of proposing all over again, of opening himself up in front of everyone here tonight. He'd risked his image, his pride, his dignity—and what had she done? She had thrown the proposal right back in his face.

'I tried to set you free tonight. I knew I couldn't tie you to a marriage to me in the way that it was going to be. I couldn't trap you like that, cage you—force you into sacrificing yourself for the country. I had to let you go, no matter how much I wanted you to stay. I had no right to impose those terms—any terms on you at all.'

'But you reinforced those terms so clearly here tonight.'

'Did I?' Alexei questioned softly. His eyes were deep pools in his drawn face. She couldn't look away if she tried. But she didn't want to try.

'My father...'

'Your father was here tonight as a free man. Did you see any chains?' he questioned sharply. 'Any armed escort?'

'No.' She had to acknowledge that. 'Then why?'

'I wanted to give your family back to you. I know what it feels like to be without a family.'

It had happened to him twice, Ria remembered. When

he had been brought to Mecjoria, supposedly to spend the
rest of his life with his father and mother reunited at last,
only to have his father die suddenly and shockingly and
then to have his parents' marriage thrown into question so
that he was rejected by the rest of the royal family. Again
when he had had his own family, with Mariette and baby
Belle. That too had ended in tragedy.

But he had talked of setting her free, and he'd wanted
to give her family back to her. None of this meant what
she had believed at first.

'I'm not sure that my father deserves your clemency,'
she said carefully. 'He has schemed against you—plotted...'

'Oh, I'll be keeping a very close eye on him from now
on,' Alexei assured her. 'For one thing I never want you to
have to deal with him again. If he tries to interfere in your
life then he will have to answer to me. Though I know
you'll be able to stand up to him for yourself from now on.
And I think the fear that he might have lost your mother
will be punishment enough. Love can do that to you.'

Love? That word again.

'I should know,' Alexei went on.

I loved once—adored her... Lost her.

'Belle...'

Alexei nodded sombrely, his eyes still fixed on her
face so that she could read his feelings in his expression.
And those thoughts made her heart contract on a wave
of painful hope. Because the look on his face now as he
looked at her was the same as when he had stared down
at the little snapshot of Belle, the person he had loved
most in all the world.

'It broke my heart to lose her. I never thought I'd feel
that way again—about anyone. But this morning when

you said that I'd trapped you, I knew I was risking losing you when I forced you into marriage.'

'For the good of the country and because you wanted me.'

She could risk saying that much. Did she dare to take it any further? He had wanted to set her free. Surely that was the act of a man who...

'And I wanted you every bit as much.' Her voice jumped and cracked as she forced herself to add more. 'I always have. I still do.'

Alexei lifted his hands, cupping her face in both of them, his lips just a breath away from hers.

'Forgive me for tonight. I tried to let you go, but I couldn't. But I thought it was worth one last try to show you that I love you and to...'

'Alexei.' Ria's hand came up to press against his mouth, stilling the rest of his words. She didn't need to hear any more. 'You love me?'

He nodded his dark head, his intent gaze never leaving hers.

'I love you. With all my heart—the heart I thought was dead when I lost little Belle. But you've brought it back to life again. You've brought me back to life. But I don't want to trap you. I don't want you here if it's not where you want to be. I'll set you free if that's what you truly want but—'

Once more she stopped his words, but this time with a wildly joyful kiss that crushed them back inside his mouth.

'That's not what I want,' she whispered against his lips. 'What I want—all I want—is right here, right now. In you.'

He closed his eyes in response to her words and she felt him draw in a deep, deep breath of release and acceptance.

'I love you,' she told him, needing to say the words, glorying in the freedom of being able to speak them out loud at last.

'And I love you. More than I can say.'

She didn't doubt it. She couldn't. She could hear it reverberate in his deep tones, in the faint tremble of the hands that held her face. It was there in his eyes, in the set of his mouth, etched into every strong muscle of his face. This was the only truth, the absolute truth. And it made her heart sing in pure joy.

'Can we start again, please?' she whispered, making each word into a kiss against his mouth. 'And if that proposal is still open…'

'It is.' It was just a sigh.

'Then I accept—freely and gladly—and lovingly. I'd be so happy to marry you and stay with you for the rest of my life.'

She was gathered up into his arms, clamped so close against his chest that she could hear the heavy, hungry pounding of his heart and knew it was beating for her. The kiss he gave her made her senses swim, her legs lose all strength so that she clung to him urgently, needing him, loving him, and knowing deep in her soul that he would always be there for her now and in the future.

It was some time before a noise from outside reminded them that everyone who had come here to attend the ball was still waiting. A thousand people, waiting to discover just what her reply had been to his proposal. Glancing towards the door, Alexei looked deep into her face and smiled rather ruefully.

'Our guests are getting impatient. We should let them in again. Let them share in our celebrations.

'But,' he added as Ria nodded her agreement, 'This will be the official celebration. The time for our private celebration will come later. I promise you that I'll make it very, very special.'

And the depth of his tone, the way he still held her close, reluctant to let go even for a moment, told Ria that it was a promise not just for tonight but for the rest of their lives together.

* * * * *

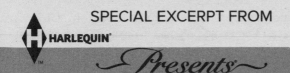
"I will not leave you again." It was a vow, accompanied by the slipping of the ring onto her finger.

Even though it was prompted by her pregnancy and the fact she now carried the heir to the Volyarus throne, the promise in his voice poured over the jagged edges of her heart with soothing warmth. The small weight of the metal band and diamonds on her finger was a source of more comfort than she would ever have believed possible.

She was not sure her heart would ever be whole again, but it did not have to hurt like it had for ten weeks.

"I won't leave you, either."

"I know." A small sound, almost a sigh, escaped his mouth. "Now we must convince your body that it still belongs to me."

"You have a very possessive side."

"This is nothing new."

"Actually, it kind of is." He'd shown indications of a possessive nature when they were dating, but he'd never been so primal about it before. "You're like a caveman."

His smile was predatory, his eyes burning with sensual intent. "You carry my child. It makes me feel *very* possessive, takes me back to the responses of my ancestors."

Air escaped her lungs in an unexpected whoosh. "Oh."

"I have read that some pregnant women desire sex more often than usual."

"I…" She wasn't sure what she felt in that department right now.

She always seemed to want him and could not imagine her hormones increasing that all too visceral need.

"However, I had not realized the pregnancy could impact the father in the same way." There was no mistaking his meaning.

Maks wanted her. And not in some casual, sex-as-physical-exercise way. The expression in his dark eyes said he wanted to devour her, the mother of his child, sexually.

Gillian shivered in response to that look.

"Cold?" he purred, pushing even closer. "Let me warm you."

"I'm not co—" But she wasn't allowed to finish the thought.

His mouth covered hers in a kiss that demanded full submission and reciprocation.

* * *

Find out what happens when this powerful prince raises the stakes of their marriage of convenience in ONE NIGHT HEIR, *out July 2013!*

And don't miss the explosive second story, PRINCE OF SECRETS, *available August 2013.*

REQUEST YOUR FREE BOOKS!

2 FREE NOVELS PLUS
2 FREE GIFTS!

YES! Please send me 2 FREE Harlequin Presents® novels and my 2 FREE gifts (gifts are worth about $10). After receiving them, if I don't wish to receive any more books, I can return the shipping statement marked "cancel." If I don't cancel, I will receive 6 brand-new novels every month and be billed just $4.30 per book in the U.S. or $4.99 per book in Canada. That's a saving of at least 14% off the cover price! It's quite a bargain! Shipping and handling is just 50¢ per book in the U.S. and 75¢ per book in Canada.* I understand that accepting the 2 free books and gifts places me under no obligation to buy anything. I can always return a shipment and cancel at any time. Even if I never buy another book, the two free books and gifts are mine to keep forever.

106/306 HDN FVRK

Name	(PLEASE PRINT)

Address	Apt. #

City	State/Prov.	Zip/Postal Code

Signature (if under 18, a parent or guardian must sign)

Mail to the **Harlequin® Reader Service:**
IN U.S.A.: P.O. Box 1867, Buffalo, NY 14240-1867
IN CANADA: P.O. Box 609, Fort Erie, Ontario L2A 5X3

**Are you a current subscriber to Harlequin Presents books
and want to receive the larger-print edition?
Call 1-800-873-8635 or visit www.ReaderService.com.**

* Terms and prices subject to change without notice. Prices do not include applicable taxes. Sales tax applicable in N.Y. Canadian residents will be charged applicable taxes. Offer not valid in Quebec. This offer is limited to one order per household. Not valid for current subscribers to Harlequin Presents books. All orders subject to credit approval. Credit or debit balances in a customer's account(s) may be offset by any other outstanding balance owed by or to the customer. Please allow 4 to 6 weeks for delivery. Offer available while quantities last.

Your Privacy—The Harlequin® Reader Service is committed to protecting your privacy. Our Privacy Policy is available online at www.ReaderService.com or upon request from the Harlequin Reader Service.

We make a portion of our mailing list available to reputable third parties that offer products we believe may interest you. If you prefer that we not exchange your name with third parties, or if you wish to clarify or modify your communication preferences, please visit us at www.ReaderService.com/consumerschoice or write to us at Harlequin Reader Service Preference Service, P.O. Box 9062, Buffalo, NY 14269. Include your complete name and address.

HP13

COMING NEXT MONTH from Harlequin Presents®
AVAILABLE JUNE 18, 2013

#3153 HIS MOST EXQUISITE CONQUEST
The Legendary Finn Brothers
Emma Darcy

The vivacious Lucy Flippence has fallen prey to
Michael Finn, whose reputation is legendary. She might
be only a tick on his to-do list, but even the luxury lifestyle
can't mask the feelings her secret has forced her to hide....

#3154 A SHADOW OF GUILT
Sicily's Corretti Dynasty
Abby Green

Valentina has always blamed Gio Corretti for her brother's
death. But when she needs help, there's only one man she
can turn to—the cold, inscrutable Gio, whose green eyes
flash with guilt, regret and a passion that calls to her.

#3155 ONE NIGHT HEIR
By His Royal Decree
Lucy Monroe

Duty comes before desire for Prince Maksim. He knew that
when he cut his ties to his mistress Gillian Harris. But when
she gets pregnant this fierce royal Cossack must claim his
heir and convince her to be his queen!

#3156 HIS BRAND OF PASSION
The Bryants: Powerful & Proud
Kate Hewitt

For billionaire Aaron Bryant, money usually solves
everything, but he's not had a problem like this before.
One unbridled night of passion with sassy Zoe Parker
has left two little lines on a test—turning both their lives
upside down.

You can find more information on upcoming Harlequin®
titles, free excerpts and more at www.Harlequin.com.

HPCNM0613RA

#3157 THE COUPLE WHO FOOLED THE WORLD
Maisey Yates

Most women would kill to be on Ferro Calvaresi's arm. But Julia Anderson is not most women. When a major deal requires these two rivals to play nicely...*together*...is the world's hottest new couple beginning to believe their own lie?

#3158 THE RETURN OF HER PAST
Lindsay Armstrong

Housekeeper's daughter Mia Gardiner knew her feelings for multimillionaire Carlos O'Connor were foolish. Until she caught the ruthless playboy's eye. Even now, older and wiser, Mia has never forgotten the feel of his touch. Then, like a whirlwind, Carlos returns....

#3159 IN PETRAKIS'S POWER
Maggie Cox

To safeguard her family's future, Natalie makes a deal with the devil—Ludo Petrakis. She must travel to Greece—as his fiancée! But seeing the cracks in Ludo's unshakable control, she finds that it gets harder to resist the smoldering tension between them....

#3160 PROOF OF THEIR SIN
One Night with Consequences
Dani Collins

Lauren is pregnant and marriage is the only way to avoid scandal, but she still bears the scars from the first time she said "I do." Can she trust the powerful but guarded Paolo enough to reveal the truth?

You can find more information on upcoming Harlequin® titles, free excerpts and more at www.Harlequin.com.

A Shadow of Guilt

* * *

Gio lifted his arms and brought his hands to Valentina's
face, cupping her jaw, his thumbs wiping away the moisture
from her cheeks. She knew she must look a sight, and Gio's
shirt had to be sodden from her tears and runny nose. But
she didn't care. A fierce burgeoning desire was rising within
her, something that had been there before but had been put
on ice for seven years.

For a long time it had been illicit and forbidden, *guilty*.
But from the moment she'd seen him again it had flamed to
life. Yet the contradiction had dueled within her: How could
she hate him and want him at the same time? But now those
questions faded in her head. *Hate* felt like a much more
indefinable thing and the desire was there, stronger than
hate, rushing through her blood and making her feel alive.

She lifted a hand and touched Gio's hard jaw. He clenched
it against her hand. Desire thickened the air around them,
unmistakable. As if questioning it, Gio looked down at her,
a small frown between his eyes. "Valentina?"

It was the same look he'd given her the other night when she'd exposed herself, and she understood it now. He'd been asking the question then, unsure of what she'd been telling him with her body language. The knowledge was heady. He *wanted* her.

One of Valentina's fingers touched Gio's bottom lip, tracing its full sensuous outline. Words were rising within her—she couldn't keep them back. "Gio…kiss me." She'd wanted this, *ached* for this for so long.

It was only after an interminable moment of nothing happening that she looked up into Gio's eyes and saw something like torture in their dark green depths. He shook his head. "This is not a good idea. You don't want this, not really."

He wanted to kiss and plunder this woman before she changed her mind, but he knew he couldn't. She hated him already; she would despise him forever for this.

Valentina's gaze narrowed on his. A light was dawning in her eyes. He braced himself for the moment when she would pull herself free and demand to know what the hell he was doing.

And then she said, "Damn you, Gio Corretti, *kiss me*."

No one can resist a Corretti!

* * *

Available July 2013 from
Harlequin® Presents® wherever books are sold.

HPEXP0613-2